SHIVER AND SPICE
Kelley St. John

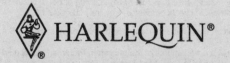

TORONTO • NEW YORK • LONDON
AMSTERDAM • PARIS • SYDNEY • HAMBURG
STOCKHOLM • ATHENS • TOKYO • MILAN • MADRID
PRAGUE • WARSAW • BUDAPEST • AUCKLAND

ISBN-13: 978-0-373-79353-2
ISBN-10:   0-373-79353-7

SHIVER AND SPICE

www.eHarlequin.com

Printed in U.S.A.

ABOUT THE AUTHOR

Kelley St. John's experience as a senior writer at NASA fueled her interest in writing action-packed suspense, although she also enjoys penning steamy romances and quirky women's fiction. Since 2000, St. John has obtained over fifty writing awards, including a National Readers' Choice Award, and was elected to the board of directors of Romance Writers of America. Visit her Web site, www.kelleystjohn.com, to learn the latest news about recent and upcoming releases and to register for fabulous vacation giveaways!

Books by Kelley St. John

HARLEQUIN BLAZE
325—KISS AND DWELL
337—GHOSTS AND ROSES

Don't miss any of our special offers. Write to us at the following address for information on our newest releases.

Harlequin Reader Service
U.S.: 3010 Walden Ave., P.O. Box 1325, Buffalo, NY 14269
Canadian: P.O. Box 609, Fort Erie, Ont. L2A 5X3

To Gayle Wilson, talented author, respected
mentor and treasured friend.

Introduction

SPICY COOKING, hot weather and sizzling sex—three of the most notable staples of life in Louisiana. Add a little voodoo, vampires and ghosts, and you've got enough to keep life interesting for several generations of Vicknairs.

Every member of this unique family can cook a mean gumbo, stay cool in thick humidity and sure enough knows how to burn up the sheets. And while they may not have had firsthand experience with voodoo and vampires— yet—they make up for it in spades with ghosts.

Currently, six Vicknair cousins are doing their part to follow family tradition, guiding lost spirits who need a little help finding the light. Obtaining their spectral assignments from grandmother Adeline, the family matriarch, even in death, the cousins generally don't have much trouble fulfilling a spirit's requirement for crossing. However, every now and then, things tend to go awry. A medium might fall in love with a spirit, the way Monique Vicknair did, or a medium's assignment may help a ghost to save a friend from a killer, which recently happened to Gage Vicknair. But what happened to

Monique and Gage isn't anything compared to what has happened to their brother, Dax.

Dax Vicknair fell in love with a spirit that was helping another to cross over. Unlike Monique's husband, who was on his way to the light when Dax's feisty sister sidetracked him, Celeste did cross over, the whole way. And now Dax is stuck over here, helping other ghosts, while the one he wants is an eternity away. Based on this assessment, Dax has determined that life, quite simply, sucks.

But everything isn't always as it seems, especially when the powers that be, and Grandma Adeline, have anything to say about it.

Prologue

CELESTE BEAUCHAMP was in the middle *again*. Where was this place, this dark room that had become her existence? And which way should she go to get out?

She stood in the center and surveyed her surroundings. A door on her left led to a pathway that she'd traveled before and that she wanted to travel again. A pathway to *him*. But that door was closed. Another door on her right was open, as it usually was, but she couldn't remember where it led. And in the center, straight ahead of her, the entire wall looked smooth and complete, but Celeste knew that the middle held a doorway too.

That door was only visible when the light came.

She held up her hand and surveyed it, glowing faintly. Her hair also shimmered, as did the rest of her body. With that center door closed tight, *she* provided the only source of light in this place.

Was she dead? Yes, she supposed she was, because a dream wouldn't be this vivid. But if she were dead, then why didn't she head on to her final destination?

Faint voices, calling her name, caused her to step toward the path to her right. Open and ready, that path would be easy to access. She'd gone there before; she remembered that much. But she never stayed there very long. She always came back here, to this middle place, because this was the way to *him*.

A soft *pop* sounded, and a pinprick of light, like a star pushing its way through a stormy cloud, pierced the middle wall and caused Celeste to turn back. It grew a bit, then a little more, until the opening was the size of a dime. Compared to the darkness around it, the radiance was exquisite, and Celeste suddenly longed to touch it. She stepped toward it, then the voices to her right screamed, and she stopped.

Rapid footsteps suddenly echoed in the confines of the room, and then a little girl bolted out of thin air and ran toward the light. Most certainly a ghost, she glowed faintly at first, but then her dress—no, her entire body—absorbed the light, until Celeste had to shield her eyes from the child's brilliance. Two pigtails of straight brown hair were capped in hot-pink bows that matched the trim on her yellow dress.

"That's it!" She clapped her hands together until the light grew into a door-size opening that illuminated the entire span of the room. "I'm going on in. Tell Prissy, my sister, to follow me. She's coming. Tell her where I am, okay?"

"Prissy?" Celeste asked, but the girl was too focused on the light to hear.

"Granny's in there. She's waiting for me. Granny, I'm coming! Oh wow, I smell cookies. Chocolate oatmeal, my favorite!" She took another step, then merged with the gleaming light.

"Wait!" Celeste shouted at the same moment that the wall absorbed the light and the girl.

She stepped forward and placed her palm where the light had been. Cold, smooth stone met her touch. She'd seen the lighted doorway before, right after the accident, but she hadn't entered it that time either. That time, another young ghost had stopped her from passing through. The girl, Chloe, needed help crossing over, and Celeste hadn't wanted to leave her behind, so she'd ignored the beckoning light and helped Chloe find her way.

That was the only time that the pathway to the left had opened, and Celeste had met Dax.

Dax. As long as she was here, in this strange middle place, she could remember him, think of him, want him. She could see the hazel eyes that had touched her soul, the sexy mouth that seemed always on the verge of a smile, those dark brown waves that framed a face full of sincerity, of kindness, and a touch of mischievousness that had made Celeste's entire body tingle.

They hadn't spoken of it before, that amazing chemistry that zinged between them, because they'd both expected her to cross over with Chloe. Plus, he was in the land of the living…and she…wasn't.

But she *didn't* cross with Chloe, and she still wasn't sure why not. Instead of entering the light, she'd gone down that path toward the voices, but that was all she recalled. And on several occasions, she'd returned here, to this middle room, in the hopes of seeing Dax again, or of finally entering the light.

Neither had happened.

Before, she didn't try to start a relationship with Dax, didn't even tell him how she felt. Why start something that they couldn't finish? But now she realized that that may have been her last chance to *really* be with a man, to be with Dax. And she'd blown it.

She wanted another shot.

Celeste hadn't had a lot of experience with men when she was living, only one relationship, and that had basically been two inexperienced teens fumbling their way through the motions. She'd always looked forward to the day when she would experience the kind of intimacy that she'd heard about, where "the earth moved." She'd certainly never had that, but she sure thought about it a lot when she was in this place. And every time she thought about it, she thought about it with one man…Dax.

She wanted to forget those voices to the right, forget that light in the middle, and head left—to Dax. She stared at the crack in the wall that identified the closed door to his world, where he could show her everything she'd never known about the desire between a man and a woman. She wanted to have that, to taste that pleasure, if only once. Was that too much to ask before she headed to the light?

"I want him," she whispered.

A loud creaking penetrated the silence, and the blocked entry to her left eased open. An elderly woman, her silver hair glowing around her shoulders, leaned out from the darkness and crooked an elegant finger toward Celeste.

"Come, *chère*. You can't stay as long as before. You're weaker now." She peered down that other path, the one with the voices, and shook her head. "Why didn't you go to them more, *chère*? You're weak because you didn't go."

Celeste looked down that darkened hall. Why would she have stayed down that path? It didn't have what she wanted. That path didn't lead to Dax.

"I wish you were stronger, *chère*, but there's nothing I can do about that now." She paused, frowned. "Still, I can let you through, but you must take care. You have to pay attention to your weakened state."

"You can take me to Dax?" Celeste asked, hurriedly moving toward the woman with the jet-black eyes and silver-white hair.

"Not me. Prissy needs your help. She's scared. And the powers that be are allowing you to help her, the way you helped Chloe, so she isn't afraid. She'll take you to Dax."

"How long?" Celeste asked, eager to see him but wanting to know the limitations. "How long can I stay?"

"It all depends, *chère*. You'll grow weaker the longer you're on that side, and with each interaction with one who's living, you'll grow weaker still. You could have been so much stronger. You've been here two months, but you didn't rest enough. You should have let them help you get stronger, instead of fighting them and staying here, in the middle." She glanced down that path with the voices again, then she quirked her mouth to the side. "My guess, *chère*, is twelve hours at best, but more likely six. It all depends on how much strength your trip takes from your spirit, and how much you interact with the living."

"Interact," Celeste repeated, then she remembered the main rule for mediums and spirits. "But we can't touch."

"A medium may not touch a spirit," the other woman said at a whisper, as though she feared someone was listening. "But there is no rule saying you cannot touch, *chère*."

Celeste swallowed as the impact of the woman's statement sank in. "I can touch him."

"Come, *chère*. Prissy needs you, and my grandson needs you too."

"Your grandson?"

"Dax. He needs you."

And that was enough for Çeleste to follow, no further questions asked.

1

Dax Vicknair carried another heavy box out of the plantation and placed it against the others already lining the majority of his brother-in-law's truck. Ryan Chappelle, the brother-in-law in question, merely shook his head and grinned.

"How much more does she have in—" He stopped speaking and hustled toward the porch, where Monique was attempting to carry a box twice her size down the stairs.

"Woman, you're going to be the death of me," Ryan groaned, taking the heavy box.

"You already died once," Dax reminded him, smirking, then turned to Monique. "You better go easy on him this time, sis. He's not ready for the light again yet."

Monique gladly let go of her end of the box and let her husband take over. She wiped her damp forehead with her palm, pushing thick blond curls away from her face. "He doesn't want me going easy on him, regarding anything," she said. "Isn't that right, dear? He likes things hard, and so do I."

Ryan's smile said way more than any words could have managed, and Dax didn't really want to hear about it anyway.

"Too much information," Dax grumbled, heading back in for another load. He paused momentarily when an echo of laughter invaded his thoughts, a little girl's laughter. He'd heard it a few times today and knew what it meant: a ghost was on the way. Probably before the day ended, he'd have a young spirit to help. Another one to help, but no one on the other side was willing to help him.

He frowned. Sure, he was mad at the powers that be for not seeming to care that he'd lost his heart to a ghost that was gone, but the little girl who'd be visiting him soon wasn't to blame. He'd have to suck it up and put on a smile, for her sake. She'd already died young; she didn't need to be faced with a pissed-off medium, too. So Dax would cheer up before she got here. Right now, however, he was going to wallow in being jealous of all the love currently surrounding him, courtesy of Monique and Ryan.

Truthfully, he wasn't bothered that his sister was so blissfully happy in marriage, or even that she was moving out of the plantation and into a home in Ormond, near her beauty salon and Ryan's new roofing job; he was bothered because he wanted a little bliss, too.

Then again, his foul mood didn't seem to dampen spirits around here. Monique and Ryan were in full newlywed mode, only a month since they tied the knot in Vegas, and Gage, Dax's older brother, had recently become engaged and was also perpetually smiling lately with his fiancée, Kayla, by his side. In short, they were all way too happy for someone who was currently in a don't-piss-me-off mood. Misery truly loves company, and so far, Dax hadn't found anyone else as...

"Listen, if you two are done with Dax, I could use his help, and I'm talking about his brain, not his brawn," Nanette said from the front door. Her arms were crossed against her chest, one foot tapped the threshold impatiently and dark brows drew together in a scowl. Clothed in a black blouse and black skinny pants, she resembled a prison guard waiting for him to enter his cell.

Dax grinned. Leave it to Nan to bring the atmosphere back down to his level. Nanette was always in semi-bitch mode. She tried to act like that was just the way she was, but Dax knew better. She was scared to death that the Vicknair family was about to lose their beloved plantation and perhaps therefore lose their ability to help the spirits, something she deemed part of the "Vicknair legacy." The home had taken a big hit from Hurricane Katrina, and the parish president, Charles Roussel, had been trying to put it on the top line of the demolition list ever since the storm. So far, they'd fought him every time, and won, every time.

Right now, however, the problem wasn't with Charles Roussel and the locals. Oh, no—in an effort to bypass Roussel's authority entirely, Nanette had decided to try to get the Vicknair plantation added to the National Register of Historic Places.

There were tons of steps involved, but Nanette thought the potential results would be worth the effort. Dax did too; he just wasn't sure what kind of chance they stood.

Truthfully, he agreed with Nan that the two of them seemed to care more about saving the house than the other Vicknair cousins. Maybe it was because she was the oldest and he was the youngest male; she felt responsible for maintaining the Vicknair legacy, and he was the last with the Vicknair name. Or maybe it was because they were the only two cousins currently residing in the plantation. Even though Nanette had told all of them that she believed they'd have a better chance of saving the place if they were all living there, the others hadn't thought it necessary and had moved on to their independence.

Jenee, the only cousin younger than Dax, actually cited the plantation as her permanent residence, but she rarely stayed there anymore. Helping to renovate the Seven Sisters Shelter in Chalmette, she tended to stay there full-time and only came back to the plantation for their traditional Saturday workdays. So basically, while the remainder of the cousins went about living their lives as usual, Nan and Dax were left to save their family home. Everyone else put in a hard day's work once a week, but as far as pulling a rabbit out of the hat with the National Historic Register, that was up to Dax and Nanette.

If they did make the cut, Roussel couldn't touch them with a ten-foot pole, which, naturally, was the goal. Problem was, Nanette had also learned that the home would stand a much better chance of making the list if it had been inhabited during the Civil War.

So far, neither Nanette, nor anyone who lived in St. Charles parish, had any proof whatsoever that the Vicknair plantation had been inhabited during the Civil War. In fact, all indications pointed to the entire family leaving to fight in the war. There weren't even references to women and children at the place in the papers on file at the parish courthouse.

But Nanette wouldn't believe that the Vicknairs had all left—who would have tended to the visiting spirits if they had? Not that she could tell the folks in charge that *that* was the reason for her doubt—and she expected Dax, known for his fascination for figuring things out, to help her prove it.

Dax had always had a knack for putting pieces of a puzzle together. When he was younger, he'd used that skill at crossword puzzles and Sudoku. Now that he was older, his primary challenges involved figuring out which prescriptions worked best for the young patients on his pediatric-pharmaceuticals route. But regardless of his puzzle-solving talents, he hadn't figured out the answer regarding the Vicknair plantation and where the family had gone during the Civil War…yet.

"I haven't found a thing on the Internet about Vicknairs living here then. And we've already checked everything at the courthouse," he said, following her through the swinging door that led to the kitchen. "The Vicknairs all headed out to support their country. Well, the Southern half of it, anyway. We're going to have to look somewhere else to find the answers."

"I know, but I have no idea where to look. There's got to be something we're missing," she said, grabbing a tall green thermos from beneath the sink. Twisting the cap off, she took the full coffeepot and poured the entire contents in.

Dax frowned. "Going somewhere?" They typically searched for information together.

"I've got parent–teacher conferences tonight. Starting in an hour. No telling how long they'll take, since we've got more ninth-graders this year than ever before, and since the majority of them feel that my first assigned essay is beyond the realm of ninth-grade history."

"What essay?"

"I'm asking them to write about their family lineage," she said. "Their Acadian ancestry in particular, if that's their history."

"In case you're wondering, I'm betting none of your students know anything about *our* ancestors living in this place during the Civil War."

"That's not the reason I—" She rolled her eyes. "Oh, all right, our current dilemma did make me wish we had better records of our family history, and I decided to help them learn their own histories too." She shrugged. "Nothing wrong with that."

"Poor kids." He dropped into a chair at the table. "And do you need the entire pot of coffee?"

She huffed out a breath, but grabbed a ceramic mug from the dish rack and poured one cup of coffee from her thermos. "Because you're helping me, I'll sacrifice a cup. And because you've been a literal pain in the ass lately." She hesitated, then added, "Listen, I know it was tough when she crossed, but brooding isn't going to help. Finding out whether this house had anybody in it during the Civil War, however, just might."

"Okay, I'll bite. How exactly is that helping me, again?"

"We both know the Vicknairs wouldn't have left this place empty. And you know that you can figure out who was here. I haven't seen a puzzle yet that you couldn't solve."

He nodded. "Right, but what has that got to do with helping me with my current situation?"

"You know, for someone so smart, sometimes it takes you a while to catch on." She took a sip from the thermos, then put the lid back on. "I'm keeping you busy, and when you're busy, you don't think about it."

"About her, you mean," he corrected. "I don't think about *her*. And you're wrong. I still think about her." He took a deep breath, exhaled.

"But?"

Dax shook his head. "Hell, you're right, to a point. Working on this house stuff is keeping my mind off of my situation, somewhat." He looked up at Nan, leaning against the counter with her thermos now tucked under one arm. "But my mind's never completely off of it, Celeste."

She frowned. "You mean Nanette."

"Right."

"At least you called me somebody that I know you like." She laughed, but Dax didn't. How was he supposed to live the rest of his life without seeing Celeste again? And hell, he never even told her how he felt.

"Dax?"

"Yeah."

"I really do appreciate you helping me with this."

"I know you do, and I appreciate your reason for trying to keep me busy. But I still think this shouldn't be a two-person show. This is their heritage too, you know." Dax knew he and Nanette were the two best suited for finding the information they needed; he simply felt like complaining about the other cousins. It was a much-needed break from brooding.

"Monique and Ryan are getting set up in their new house, and Ryan's starting his new roofing job, so they're busy. Tristan is working at the firehouse. Between her college classes and trying to raise money for the Seven Sisters Shelter, Jenee doesn't have time to help. And…"

"And?"

"And they aren't really your problem. You've got to get over it—get over *her*—on your own. Get your mind on something else. Sure, working on finding our house's history will help, but why don't you go out, too. Before this summer, you were out with someone different all the time. You haven't even been on a date since she left, have you?"

"Your point?"

"Half the women in the parish would jump at the chance to go out with you, and you're sitting around in an eternal stag mode, pining over a woman you can never have. I think it's about time you got out of that self-induced funk."

"I sure hope you're kinder to your students." He took a big sip of coffee and enjoyed the strong taste of chicory on his tongue.

"Nope, I pretty much lay it all on the line." She smiled, and Dax couldn't help but reciprocate. Nanette had one of those killer grins that just made him feel better, even if he really wasn't in the mood to feel all that much better now.

He took another sip of coffee and could already feel the strong surge of caffeine giving him a jolt.

"You know, you could go out tonight, and then search for more information later," she said. "There are a couple of teachers at the high school who have asked if you're still avail—"

Dax held up a hand. He didn't want to be fixed up, especially not with Nanette's coworkers. It'd be way too easy for her to get the sordid details, and he wasn't about to be high-school teacher lounge fodder. More than that, he could have a date every night of the week, with a different female every night, and could damn well get lucky each and every time…and it wouldn't help. That was another reason for his current state of frustration. He needed a good all-night bout of hot and heated, wild and wicked, no-holds-barred sex, but he didn't want it with anyone except Celeste. And he'd never even touched her.

But he'd sure dreamed about touching her, and doing a lot of other things to her, too. How was he supposed to move on to breathing females, when he had it so bad for a ghost? And a crossed-over one at that?

"Just so you know," he said, "I've got a spirit coming, so I probably don't need to go out tonight, and I'm not sure how much time I'll have to search for Civil War Vicknairs."

There, maybe *that'd* get Nanette off his back about dating, or lack thereof.

As he suspected, word of a ghost coming got her attention. She placed her thermos on the counter. "You've got a spirit on the way? Boy or girl?"

Even though they'd never officially decided to specialize in certain spirits, each Vicknair cousin always seemed to get the same type of ghostly visitors. Dax, for example, typically helped children to cross over. Now was no exception. The soft giggles he'd heard all day confirmed that a little girl was on her way. "Girl."

"I haven't had an assignment in three months," Nan said, her disappointment evident.

"Maybe Grandma Adeline is giving you a break until the school year is further along. The beginning is always the most difficult for you, isn't it? When you're starting to learn the new students and all?" he said. Nanette tended to worry more than the other cousins when she went too long without being asked to help a ghost cross over. Dax suspected that she actually judged her self-worth by the number of ghosts she helped to cross. Oddly enough, she was happier when she got a visit from a ghost in trouble. It wasn't that she liked knowing the ghost was having a hard time; it was simply that she liked helping. That was just the way she was, and was probably the reason she'd gone into teaching in the first place.

"Maybe," she said, still frowning.

"Anyway, I've got a little girl coming, so I'll search the Net for more information until she gets here, but once she does, I'll need to spend my time with her."

"Of course." Nanette picked her thermos back up, glancing at the clock. "Ghosts always come first, and maybe I'll get another one soon."

Dax nodded, knowing that Nanette would be thrilled to cut parent–teacher conferences short in order to help a spirit. But if she hadn't heard thunder today, her sign that spirits were on the way, it probably wasn't going to happen anytime soon.

He held up his mug as she started to pass, and she topped off his coffee. Then the giggling got louder, and he closed his eyes to hear the little girl.

"Your ghost?" Nanette asked.

"Yeah."

"You should go see if you have a letter yet," she said, referring to the lavender-tinted notes their grandmother sent from the other side to inform them of their medium assignments. The envelopes were always left in the same place, on the silver tea service in the sitting room, and would tell Dax the identity, and the requirement for crossing, of the child whose giggle had overpowered his thoughts.

"Go on," Nanette instructed. "Don't worry about searching for information now. If you get more time later, then you can try to find something."

The laughter got louder, and he stood. "I think you're right." Finishing off his cup of coffee, he placed his mug in the sink. "I may already have a letter."

Nanette crossed the kitchen and hugged him, and his face was suddenly smothered in her thick black hair. "Tell me all about her when I get back," she said, then turned and exited through the back door.

Dax watched her climb into her old red Camaro, and smiled. The Vicknairs may not have a lot of money to spare, with every dime going into keeping the house from falling in, but even if they didn't drive the newest cars around, they sure enough drove the coolest. Or in Nan's case, the fastest.

He watched her head out, leaving a cloud of dust in her wake, then examined the sky. It was growing darker as late afternoon turned to evening, and he hoped that his ghost would show soon. He'd always had a soft spot for kids, whether they were breathing or not.

Dax exited the kitchen, then made his way up the stairs to the rose-tinted sitting room. The tea service was void of an envelope, but he'd barely crossed the room when a pale purple letter materialized in its center.

"Perfect timing," he said, stepping forward to verify

the fact that the name on the outside, written in his grandmother's swirling script, was his.

Dax.

Adeline Vicknair's favorite scent, magnolia, wafted from the stationery. Sitting down on the red velvet settee, Dax picked up the envelope, and the giggles in his head immediately ceased. He opened it and withdrew the usual three sheets of paper composing a medium's assignment. The top one, on pale purple stationery with a scalloped border, was his grandmother's letter.

Dax read the information at the top of the page.

Name of Deceased—Priscilla "Prissy" Fontenot.

Reason for Death—Car accident.

The bottom of the page identified what the young spirit had to do to cross over.

Requirement for Passage—Making sure her father is okay and telling her parents goodbye.

Dax nodded at the familiar requirement. Often, particularly in the case of an accident, a ghost would want to let the person who felt responsible for their death know that they weren't hurting on the other side, that they were, in fact, in a better place and that they would see each other again. What's more, a ghost could view those they were close to on this side from the other realm. That fact always seemed to ease the minds of the loved ones who remained here.

Dax frowned. Ghosts could see individuals that they

were close to on this side. Could Celeste see him? Did she ever try? And would he be able to sense her watching? Surely he would sense *something* if she were, wouldn't he? But he hadn't felt her at all, not since the day she left.

Frustrated with that realization, he dropped the purple page on the couch, then moved to the second sheet. As usual, it listed rules for dealing with the spirits. Naturally, he knew them all, but since he was required to read the pages in their entirety before his assignment officially began, he read them again. They were pretty basic. Take care of the spirit's needs in a timely manner, don't abuse the bonding that occurs between medium and spirit, and don't touch a spirit.

He dropped the sheet of rules on top of the first page and moved to the final page, the official document directing his grandmother to assign Prissy Fontenot to one of her grandchildren. His assignment, like the rules, was straightforward and to the point. Basically, he had one day to make sure the young spirit took care of her business on this side and headed toward the light.

One day. Not much time for visiting, but the spirits seemed to know best when it came to ghostly requirements for crossing. Maybe the little girl would get too attached if she spent longer with her parents before crossing, and then find it harder to go to the light. Or maybe someone was waiting for her on the other side, and she needed to get there quickly. There were all types of reasons that the powers that be could have given Priscilla—Prissy—Fontenot such a short time to fulfill her requirement for crossing. But at least the requirement was an easy one, and one Dax could help her with in a prompt manner.

If she only had to see that her father was okay and say goodbye to her parents before she crossed, Dax could tell her how to visit them. They wouldn't be able to see her, of course, but they'd still feel her presence. Once she saw they were all right, she would immediately cross over.

He refolded the pages and tucked them back in the envelope. How long before the little girl showed?

"We're here," a small voice whispered from behind him.

Dax's first thought was...*we?* Then he turned and saw a tiny girl, smiling softly, with a beautiful golden-haired beauty holding her hand.

Celeste.

Her hair was as long as he remembered, the blond spirals touching her waist. Last time he'd seen her, she'd been wearing a yellow tank top and jeans, but now she wore a loose white gown that barely clung to her shoulders and was so sheer, he could almost—almost—see if she was a real blonde.

A whirlwind of questions cluttered Dax's mind. How was she here? And why? Hadn't she crossed already? And why was her clothing different? Because she'd crossed over entirely? Or was it something else?

Was she even here? Or was his mind merely seeing what he wanted—desperately wanted—to see.

She smiled, and Dax knew this was no fantasy. She was here. His ghost *had* returned.

"Celeste."

2

DURING EACH of her trips to that middle room, Celeste had dreamed of seeing Dax again, had planned what she'd say, what she'd do. Now that he was right in front of her, her throat was dry, her knees were weak, and her entire body burned to get closer, closer to the only man who'd truly touched her heart, so much that even on the other side, she hadn't been willing to let his memory go.

And she could touch him.

Celeste ached to reach for him, to run her fingers down the strong features of his face, brush her mouth across his and get to know him in the most intimate of ways, but she still didn't know if he felt for her what she felt for him. And she suspected that Dax had no idea that the no-touching rule didn't apply to spirits.

The tiny girl beside her squeezed Celeste's hand and reminded her of the main reason she couldn't act on impulse right now. She couldn't even attempt to confront whatever existed between the two of them until they took care of Prissy.

"Celeste?" Dax's hazel eyes were as mesmerizing as

she remembered, dark brown lashes further emphasizing the golden flecks around their center. Those eyes drew her in, held her captive. He looked so good, so real, so *alive*. And there was something deeper in those eyes, an intensity that she believed she recognized and understood. *Desire*. The way he was looking at her...was exactly the way she was feeling toward him. As though he couldn't wait to get as close as possible, and to do all of the things they hadn't done before.

She forced herself to swallow, then nodded.

"You—haven't crossed," he said, his head shaking slightly as he made the statement, as though it wasn't possible that she was standing in his grandmother's sitting room, in the very place where she'd met him before, with another little girl by her side.

"No, I haven't."

"Why didn't you?" he asked, stepping toward her, and one corner of his mouth quirked up in that semi-smile she remembered. She licked her lips and imagined teasing that sexy smile with her tongue. There were so many things she wanted to try, wanted to do.

"I've wanted you—wanted to see you—again." His head shook again, still apparently trying to determine how she'd returned. "Where have you been?"

She wished she could give him an answer. "I don't know."

Evidently tired of listening to the adults and ready to get to her own mission, Prissy tugged at Celeste's arm. "Is that him? Are you Dax? The one who'll take me to

Daddy? I need to make sure he's okay, and I want to tell him and Mama goodbye."

Celeste tried to focus on the little girl and not on Dax, but Adeline Vicknair's words kept whispering in her thoughts.

"Twelve hours at best, but more likely six."

She didn't have time to waste, but they had to help Prissy get to her parents. What if that took all the time she had? And what if she never could get back again? She wanted to talk to Dax, really get to know him, learn as much as possible about him before she crossed. And she wanted to make love with him.

"You'll help me?" Prissy asked, and Celeste put her own fears at bay. Hopefully, she'd still have at least a bit of time left after they helped the little girl. Maybe not enough to experience everything she wanted to, but she wasn't going to worry about that now. She had another chance to be with Dax, and she was grateful for whatever time they got. As soon as they took care of Prissy, she'd spend every minute, every second, with him.

"Yes, I'll help you," Dax said to Prissy, then he gave Celeste a soft smile. "I can't believe you're here. I thought—well, I didn't think I'd see you again. There's so much I want to say, but—" he looked at Prissy and smiled at the eager expression on her face "—I need to get you to your folks first, don't I?"

She nodded, and Dax crouched down to eye level with her. Then he looked up toward Celeste. "You're here? I mean, you aren't leaving anytime soon?"

"Six to twelve hours," she said honestly.

His smile slipped, but then he nodded. "I'll take what I can get." Then he turned his attention back to Prissy. "I will help you see your parents again, okay?"

She nodded enthusiastically. "Okay."

Celeste noted how at ease Dax was with the little ghost. He obviously knew that crouching to her level would make her more comfortable; he was the type of guy who would remember those kind of little things, the type of guy who paid attention to details. Celeste wondered if that trait carried over to other aspects of his life. Was he always that in tune with what people needed? Would he be that in tune to what his lover needed?

She swallowed. Yes, he would.

She could hardly wait.

Prissy, oblivious to the sensual tension filling the room, rattled, "My sister, Cassie, she went over already, you know, to see Granny. But I just want to see Mama and Daddy one more time, and maybe hug them, if I can. Can I?"

"Yes," Dax said, his voice thick with emotion—for the little ghost, or for Celeste? Or both?

"Ms. Adeline said you can help me get back to them. I was scared to come down the dark path at first, but then Ms. Adeline found Celeste, and she kept me from being afraid."

"I'm glad she did," he said, then those hazel eyes focused on Celeste once more. "Very glad." There was no denying that his words were spoken more to Celeste than to Prissy, and the desire in his tone was unmistakable.

"Do you know them? My daddy and mama? My daddy's name is Stanton, and my mama's name is Rebecca." Prissy's pigtails bobbed with every word.

She wore clothing similar to what her twin had been wearing, except where hot-pink bows had adorned Cassie's head, bright yellow ones topped off Prissy's brown hair. And where Cassie's dress had been yellow trimmed in pink, Prissy's was hot pink trimmed in yellow. Celeste imagined the twins together, in their matching dresses and identical angelic faces, and was sure that, in their parents' minds, they were unique treasures.

Celeste wondered where they had been going when they died. They were dressed up, maybe for church?

She glanced down at the glowing white satin gown that covered her body. Last time she came to Dax, she'd had on the jeans and tank that she'd been wearing when the bus crashed. Why had she changed? And how?

Prissy continued talking, but Celeste wasn't listening; she was surveying the way the young girl's body glowed. A bright, almost golden-yellow light illuminated Prissy's entire body; in contrast, Celeste's body was cloaked in a pale, creamy luminance.

Was the difference because she was an adult, and Prissy a child? Or was there more to it?

Prissy's sobs quickly yanked her away from her thoughts. "I miss them."

Celeste's heart ached for the little girl's parents, specifically for her father, who Adeline had said was driving the car when it crashed.

"Can you see them now?" Dax leaned toward the girl, but didn't reach out to touch her, Celeste noticed. She wondered if that was why she'd been called to help Prissy, and Chloe, with crossing. Right now, as Dax spoke to the little girl, her hand gripped Celeste's, as though she was fearful to let go. It had to be scary for these young children to try to complete these tasks on their own. Even with a medium to help, they'd need someone who could hold their tiny hand, someone... like Celeste. She returned Prissy's squeeze and smiled down at the little girl.

Prissy nodded at Dax. "I saw them as soon as we got here," she said. "Right after Celeste and I left Ms. Adeline and then came here, I could see them. And I need to talk to them."

"Where are they?" Dax asked, still at Prissy's eye level.

"At the hospital," she said, her black eyes glittering. "Ms. Adeline said to tell you it's the one where your brother works. That's where Daddy is."

Dax nodded. "Where Gage works. That's Ochsner, in New Orleans. Tell me something, Prissy. Can you still see them, right now? Because if you can see your parents now, you can go to them at the hospital. All you have to do is think about wanting to be with them, and you'll go directly to that room. You can stay beside them and try to comfort them."

"But they won't know I'm there," she said. "Not unless you come too, so you can tell them."

"Some people don't realize when a spirit is near, but most do, particularly if it's someone they care about and love, the way your parents love you."

"But I need you to come, so I'm sure that they know I'm there. I want them to know," she said, her small face set with fierce determination.

"I'm going to leave right now to go to the hospital," he assured. "But Ochsner is a good hour's drive from here, so it'll take me a little time to get there. If you want to come with me in my car, you can, or you can go on ahead and stay with them, until I get there. When I'm there, I'll help you communicate with them."

"Then I can talk to them, you mean?"

He smiled. "Yes."

"Okay. Then I'd like to go to them now, please," she said, and tilted her head toward Celeste. "You'll come too, won't you?"

"Of course I will. I won't leave you," Celeste said calmly, though her emotions were in turmoil. An hour's drive. Another hour of her time with Dax.

Prissy turned back to Dax. "So we'll see you in an hour, right?"

"I'll see you in an hour." He stood and looked pointedly at Celeste. "Six to twelve hours, right?"

"That's what Adeline said."

His smile faltered slightly. "Okay. Then we'll make the most of them."

"Yes." She swallowed. "Dax, after we help Prissy…"

He waited. When she didn't continue, he prompted, "After we help Prissy…"

"I need you—"

"Come on, I see them!" Prissy excitedly pulled on Celeste's hand. The two of them instantly left the plantation, and Dax, and arrived at the hospital room.

Prissy ran to the man in the bed, and the woman sitting at his side, while Celeste's head reeled from the rapid change in scenery. Her body suddenly felt as if she'd run a marathon. She moved to the opposite side of the room, found a chair and sat down. She was exhausted, already tired and drained from her brief time here, and she hadn't even touched Dax yet.

She had an hour before he would arrive at the hospital, and she needed to rest while Prissy spent time with her parents. Otherwise, she might not have the strength to even talk to Dax again, much less anything else.

Dax. She'd been prepared to tell him that she needed him to help her, too, to show her how everything could be between a man and a woman, when they truly bonded, truly joined souls. Prissy's exclamation had halted her midsentence. But really, she didn't need any more words. Those three said it all.

I need you.

3

"CELESTE. CELESTE, wake up." Dax's voice echoed in her thoughts, and she opened her eyes to see him looking down at her. His hands were on the armrests of the hospital chair and he leaned above her, so close, but not nearly close enough.

"Is she okay? I just thought she was tired," Prissy said, moving from her spot beside her father's bed to stand by Celeste's chair.

"You're all right?" he asked Celeste, tilting his head as he looked into her eyes.

"Yes," she said. "I guess I was more tired than I thought."

"Who's Celeste?" Prissy's mother asked Dax. She looked past him to what must have appeared to her eyes to be an empty chair.

"Someone else is here?" Prissy's father asked from the bed.

Dax's dark brows furrowed. "I'll be right back." Then he moved away from Prissy and Celeste and briefly explained to the little girl's parents about the spirit that had accompanied their daughter to this side.

Prissy scooted closer to Celeste and excitedly chatted nonstop while he was speaking. "Dax said he'd never seen a ghost sleep before. He tried to wake you up when he first got here, but you were so sound asleep that he decided to let you rest while he talked to my mama and daddy, because he said you must be tired. Guess what, they can *feel* me when I touch them. Did you know that? Isn't that amazing? And now they know that I'm okay, and that Cassie's okay." She tilted her head. "You are just tired, right? You're not sick or anything, are you? You've been asleep a long time."

"No," Celeste said. "I'm not sick." Could ghosts even get sick? She didn't know. If asked before now, she'd have said they couldn't, but she'd also have wagered that ghosts didn't sleep. And she'd been asleep...*a long time?* "How long? Prissy, how long did I sleep?" she asked, unable to control the tinge of panic in her tone.

How much time had she lost?

"I don't know," Prissy looked up at Dax, who'd returned to stand beside her. "She wants to know how long she slept."

"Just long enough for me to drive here and talk with Prissy's folks. An hour and a half, I'd say. Celeste, *are* you okay?"

She nodded. She did feel better now, though she was disappointed that some of her precious time on this side had been wasted. Celeste glanced out the hospital window to see that it was now dark, definitely evening.

When they'd arrived here, there had been some daylight outside; she was sure of it. "What time is it now, Dax? How much time do we have before I have to leave?"

"It's just past eight. You and Prissy got to the plantation around six," he said. "So, based on what you told me, midnight at the earliest, or six in the morning at the latest."

"I hope it's the latest," she said and was rewarded with one of his sexy grins.

"Trust me, I do too."

She straightened in the chair, and he backed away, giving her room to stand, being careful not to touch her while she did.

"You're sure you're okay?" he repeated.

"Yes, much better now." She was telling the truth. That nap had given her more energy, and she was grateful for that, even if it did use up some of her time. Besides, Dax had been en route to the hospital, so that was the perfect opportunity to rest.

"You'll grow weaker the longer you're on that side, and with each interaction with one who's living, you'll grow weaker still. It all depends on how much strength your trip takes from your spirit, and how much you interact with the living."

Was Celeste weak from the initial trip to this side, or was she weak from interacting with Dax? She prayed it was the trip. Because they'd barely interacted at all…yet.

"Are you leaving?" Prissy asked.

Dax nodded. "Yes, but you can stay with your folks until it's time for you to cross."

"Prissy's staying with us a while?" her father asked. His face was bruised from the accident, and a line of stitches creased his right brow, but he still managed a smile at the thought of having one of his daughters with him a little longer, even if only in spirit.

"Prissy was given a day to visit with you, and at the end of that time, she'll cross. But until then, she can stay with both of you here," Dax said.

"Thank you. Thank you for letting us know that she and Cassie are okay, and will be okay until we see them again," her mother said, her voice quivering as she spoke.

Prissy moved back by the bed and kissed her father's cheek. He moved his hand to the very spot she'd touched. "I feel her." Then the little girl turned to her mother and hugged her. The woman closed her eyes and whispered, "I do too."

"We'll leave you alone now." Dax moved toward the door and Celeste followed.

They'd barely shut the door when he said, "Come on, I don't want to waste any of our time." He turned and started down the hallway, darting his attention from room to room, until finally, at the end of the hallway, he found what he was evidently looking for, an unoccupied hospital room. "In here."

Celeste followed him inside, then watched him lock the door. Turning, he thoroughly inspected her, starting with her face, then down her glowing body.

"You're really here."

She could see the questions, the confusion, clearly in

his eyes. He had no idea how she'd returned, or whether she'd be able to come back again, and unfortunately, neither did she. But Celeste didn't want to waste time trying to figure it out. She didn't want to return to the middle with regrets over not telling him what she so desperately wanted him to know. "Dax, I—"

"Wait." He still leaned against the door, as if he suspected that somehow someone would come in and ruin this moment, this perfect moment, with the two of them together, and completely alone. Celeste felt the same way. She was finally with him, and it seemed, indeed was, too good to be true. Eventually, she'd be pulled away again. The impulse to simply grab him, kiss him, be with him, was so strong…but the impulse to tell him everything she was feeling, everything she'd felt for him since she'd left last time, was equally strong.

His voice was deep and urgent as he spoke. "I know you said you should be here for hours, but I don't want to bank on anything. There's something I've wanted to tell you, something I should have said the last time, before you left in the summer."

Celeste knew it wasn't possible, but she could swear that she felt her heart racing as he spoke.

"Celeste, I haven't stopped thinking of you. I've wanted to kick myself for not taking advantage of the days we had together. That week with you and Chloe, well, it meant more to me than any other assignment I've had, not only because we helped Chloe cross over, but because I spent those days with you, getting to know you, being around you, watching you with Chloe…and feeling you with me." Dax swallowed, and his jaw tensed before he spoke again. "The last two months, since you left, I've been a real ass to be around." He gave her that crooked grin. "Just ask my cousins. Hell, I thought you were gone, crossed over, completely. And I didn't think you could come back after you crossed."

"I don't think I could have come back, if I had crossed over. But I didn't."

"Why not?" he asked, then smiled again, and again, she sensed her pulse racing. "And just so you know, I'm asking so we can try to keep it from happening. I *don't* want you to cross Celeste. We haven't had enough time together, not nearly enough."

She looked down to verify that she was, indeed, still glowing, still a spirit instead of living, breathing flesh and bones. To her dismay, the glow was definitely still there, and even a little brighter than before, more pale yellow than creamy white. She frowned.

"What is it?" Dax asked. "Tell me."

"For a moment, I thought that maybe—maybe I was alive again." She looked back up and was touched by the heartfelt emotion in those hazel eyes. "But that isn't possible, is it?"

"If it is, I'll find a way to make it happen. I swear it. And trust me, I'm a firm believer, especially now, that you can't rule out anything about the other side." He stepped away from the door and moved closer to Celeste, so close that she could feel his breath against her lips.

"How can I keep you here, or how can I help you come back again? Just tell me, before you have to go. I don't want to lose you again."

"Dax," she whispered. "I—I don't know why I didn't cross. Part of me feels like it's because my spirit simply wasn't ready to head to the light, but another part thinks that…"

"What?" he asked, so close now that she could see his pulse throbbing solidly at his throat.

She licked her lips and thought of how that pulse would feel against her mouth. "Part of me feels like I didn't cross because I couldn't leave you."

The pulse at his throat grew quicker still, and Celeste couldn't hold back anymore. She longed for him to move even closer, for that sexy mouth to touch hers, and then for his body to touch her, truly touch her, from head to toe, so that no part of her wasn't completely engulfed by Dax. She burned to feel even more, to have him inside of her, filling her, making her complete just once before she had to cross again.

"Dax, I know you can't touch me," she whispered, "but those rules don't apply to me. And I've been aching for this." Her hand trembled as she tenderly brought her fingertips to his cheek.

Heat, powerful scorching heat seared through her body the moment she touched him, warming her, filling her, exciting her. She eased her hand along his face and reveled in the coarse stubble against the pads of her fingertips. Each and every sensation fueled her desire.

She didn't know what was happening, didn't understand how merely touching him caused her to gasp, made her chest clench tight, and created an intense spiraling need deep within her core…but it did. And she didn't want to stop.

"Celeste." His voice was a low, guttural growl. Whatever was happening wasn't one-sided, and the knowledge that she was having the same effect on him added even more fuel to the flame.

"I want you," she said, moving her hands to the buttons on his shirt. She fumbled with the first one, and then the second, while Dax's hands fisted at his sides.

"I want—I need to touch you, Celeste," he said, and she saw his hands open, then reach toward her.

She swallowed, shook her head. "No, Dax, please. Don't. Don't do anything that could cause them to make me leave. I can touch you. Just let me touch you, just once." Her hands continued to move down the buttons on his shirt, while his clenched into tight fists again.

"Hell, Celeste, I want you too."

She pulled the two sides of his shirt apart and slid her palms against his solid chest, then she leaned toward him, rested her head against his warmth and watched the way her glowing hair shimmered beside his muscled flesh. His heart pounded fiercely, and she took pleasure in the steady vibration that emphasized the life still bristling within him. She wanted to feel that way again, wanted to feel alive again, and she believed she knew how to make that happen. "I want to make love to you, Dax, before I go."

She turned her head and kissed the pulse in his neck, and felt the hardness of his erection against her stomach.

Her skin was on fire, her body burning, needing and determined...but something else was joining in the flurry of emotions she was experiencing, and Celeste recognized it with a sudden pang of fear. "No," she whispered as her energy started to drain, and her body began glowing brighter.

The door to the room shook, and a female voice called from the other side, "Hello? Is someone in there? We need this room." Then the woman cleared her throat and yelled, "Can you bring me the keys?"

Dax's curse was softly spoken against her hair. "Damn. We've got to go somewhere else, Celeste."

"I—" She struggled to form the words, but it was getting harder and harder to concentrate, and harder to move away from Dax, and from the heat he generated within her. "I can't."

He looked down at her, and the desire in his eyes quickly converted to concern. "Celeste. What's happening?"

She glanced at her hands against his chest, and they were painfully bright now, almost as bright as Cassie had been right before she stepped into the light. And she was so very tired. "Need to rest," she said, and felt the truth of the statement. If she didn't rest, she feared that she might have no choice but to head toward the light; she might not have the strength to fight it. But if she rested, she lost more time with Dax.

Celeste felt her spirit begin to fade. But it wasn't time yet. Six hours at least; that's what Adeline had guessed, but it hadn't nearly been six hours yet.

"Don't leave, Celeste. Fight it," he said. "Stay with me."

"Need to rest a while," she whispered, but the words were slurred as her spirit pulled at her to leave the room.

The lock to the door turned, and Dax quickly asked, "Where? Where are you going?"

"Plantation." It was the only place she could think of to go, and the only word she managed to say before she suddenly found herself on the velvet settee in Adeline's sitting room. There she closed her eyes and prayed for enough energy to do…everything she wanted before her time ran out completely.

THE DOOR TO the hospital room opened, and a scowling nurse barreled in. "Excuse me, but did you not *hear* me knocking?" she snapped. "We need this room."

"Right, I'm leaving," Dax said, pushing by her and catching a glimpse of a gurney, evidently the patient they were wheeling in, as he darted past. Celeste was on her way to the plantation to rest, if the powers that be didn't yank her all the way back. "She'd better be there," he said to the ceiling, knowing that the guys above were undoubtedly listening. He spent every waking moment never knowing when he'd get called to help a spirit, never knowing when he'd get called to help *them*, and right now he needed a little reciprocation. He wanted the powers that be to help Celeste stay on this side, at the bare minimum for the six hours she'd been promised.

He could still feel her touch on his face, against his chest. The way her fingers had trembled, and the way she'd rubbed her body against his as she laid her head on his chest. He wanted to feel *all* of her against him, and he'd better get a chance to feel it before the day ended. "I mean it," he added, sprinting down the hallway and toward the parking deck. "She'd better be there."

He rounded a corner and ran slap into his older brother.

"Hey man, where's the fire?" Gage Vicknair grabbed him by the shoulders and halted his progress. He had a stethoscope slung around his neck, a hospital badge clamped to the pocket of his navy scrubs and a look of exhaustion on his face. "One of the interns said she thought she saw my brother up here, but she didn't say he was running a race. What's happening?"

"Can't talk," Dax said breathlessly. "I've gotta get home." Then he thought about the little ghost visiting with her parents in the hospital room nearby. "Listen. My current assignment, a little ghost named Prissy Fontenot, is here at the hospital in her father's room."

"She's visiting him before she crosses?"

Dax nodded, eager to leave and get to Celeste, but also wanting to make sure that Prissy's needs were taken care of. "I'm sure she'll be fine staying with them until she has to cross over, but would you mind checking in and just making sure that everything, well, seems okay with them? They can sense her, so they should know when she crosses. And if they do need me for anything, call me and let me know."

"Yeah, I can watch her, but why aren't you staying with them?" Gage asked.

"It's Celeste. She's back. She came back with Prissy, but we don't have long."

"The ghost from the summer?" Gage looked confused. "I thought she crossed over."

"I thought so too, but she's back, for a little while. And I've got to go. No time to explain now." He darted on down the hall, but heard his brother calling after him.

"Did you tell Celeste that she's made you a royal pain in the ass to be around since she left?"

Dax didn't bother stopping to let him know that he had, in fact, told her that, but he still had plenty more to tell her. And plenty more to do with her before she crossed, if they could.

"Those rules don't apply to me. And I've been aching for this."

She could touch him. That fact alone shocked the hell out of him, but the way her body trembled when she touched him, the way her silver-gray eyes deepened to charcoal—that evidence of how touching him affected her—*that* had made him harder than he'd ever been in his life.

Dax wanted in her, to be a part of her before she had to leave again.

What if she never came back?

No. He couldn't worry about that now. He climbed

into his car, cranked it and glanced at the digital clock on the dash: *9:28*.

He'd be home in an hour, earlier if he sped, which he would. Seconds were priceless now, and he resented each and every one he wasn't with Celeste. The fact that she'd already had to rest twice told him that they probably wouldn't get anywhere near twelve hours together on this side. Midnight was probably as good as it'd get; that was only two and a half hours away, and the majority of one of those hours would be spent driving, trying to get to her.

Then again, after she rested before, she'd felt better, and was able to touch him.

But why was she so tired, anyway? Why *would* a ghost be tired? Something wasn't right, something that Dax couldn't put his finger on.

He hurriedly left the parking deck, his Beemer catching a wheel as he jerked the car onto Jefferson Highway. He punched the accelerator and the car jumped to life. Dax was extremely thankful his company hadn't skimped on his corporate car. Right now he needed speed, and—as his speedometer neared a hundred—he had it at his fingertips.

Now, as long as he didn't meet any cops between the hospital and the plantation, he'd be there soon. And he and Celeste could pick up where they'd left off in that hospital room…

4

THE SOUND of a slamming door roused Celeste from her sleep. She opened her eyes prepared to be surrounded by the cold darkness of the middle room. But she wasn't in darkness, she wasn't cold and she wasn't in the middle room.

Instantly, she remembered where she was, and why. She was in Adeline Vicknair's sitting room, its hues of rose and pink a welcome change from what she'd been anticipating. And she was here because she'd been given another chance to see Dax. She looked toward the tall grandfather clock centered between the room's two heavily draped windows. Fifteen minutes past ten. Less than two hours until midnight. Would she get longer than Adeline's estimate?

Would she get less?

Would she get a chance to be with Dax, *really* be with him, before she had to leave?

Pounding footsteps echoed outside the door of the sitting room, and Celeste held her breath, hoping that the person so eagerly charging up the stairs was...

"Dax."

His brown waves were tousled, his hazel eyes were intense and eager, and his breathing was heavy, loud enough for her to hear him exhale when he saw her. "You're here."

"I told you I would be," she said, though she'd also wondered whether the powers that be would allow her to stay, after she'd become so exhausted at the hospital. She watched him enter the room, muscles flexing under his shirt, legs moving purposefully toward her, sexy mouth promising to please, and she was very, very grateful to whoever had decided to let her stay on this side a little longer.

He stopped next to the settee and looked down at her, then toward the clock. "We don't have long, Celeste."

"I know." She stood and took a tiny step, closing the gap between them. "And I don't know whether I'll have another chance to be with you, Dax. I don't know if I'll make it back, once I leave again."

"I'll find a way," he promised.

She smiled. "I'm sure if you can, you will, but just in case this is my last time here, I want to know..." She brushed back the brown waves at his temple, then slid her fingers through his hair.

The sizzling bolt of electricity that rocketed through her was even stronger than last time, even more potent.

"What do you want to know?" he asked, those eyes gazing into hers while she attempted to control the maddening, exhilarating rush from touching him.

She examined the golden flecks in the middle of the

brown and green. She wanted to remember the uniqueness of them, the uniqueness of *him*, beyond the middle realm.

"Tell me, Celeste. Whatever you want to know, whatever you want to do," he urged.

Her mouth was dry and her center burned for something that she'd never had. She licked her lips, and forced her throat to work. "I've been with a man before—" she smiled softly "—or rather, I've been with a boy."

Those gorgeous eyes widened, but he didn't speak.

She cleared her throat. "I've never been with anyone who knew—really knew—how to please a woman." Celeste moistened her lips again. "I want to experience that before I cross, Dax. And I want it to be with someone I care about, someone who makes me feel things I've never felt before, the way I feel when I merely touch you."

"I wanted you this summer," he said, his voice raspy with desire. "And I've wanted only you since you left."

She pushed her fingers through his hair, relishing the feel of the coarse strands tickling her palm. Then she moved her hands to the top of his shirt and unbuttoned the top two buttons. Then, too eager to wait until the rest were undone, she slid them inside, running her palms across the broadness of his chest, then finding his flat nipples and circling them with her fingertips.

"I want to touch you," he said. "So bad it hurts."

With her lips a mere fraction from his, she smiled, and continued circling his nipples with her fingers. Odd, how exciting it was to feel them harden beneath her command. "I know you do, and I know that this would be easier if you could, since you obviously know more about where to touch, and where to be touched, than I do." She gently pushed against his chest, guiding him back until he sat down on the settee. "So I suppose you'll have to tell me what to do." She did her best to sound confident, assured and ready to do…anything he instructed.

"Tell you what to do," he repeated, and she noticed that he shoved his hands between the cushions on the settee, apparently not trusting himself to control them.

"Yes," she said, and her voice was deeper, richer with her desire. But she was also feeling something equally as potent; her body growing weak. Consumed with passion, but weak with exhaustion. She prayed that passion would win out this time, at least long enough to…

She lowered herself in front of him, moving her body between his legs. The hard bulge that distended his jeans was undeniable, and she wanted to feel that part of him, with her hands, then with her mouth, and then inside of her. "Tell me what to do," she said again, then she looked at him, and lost all fear. "Tell me," she repeated.

He leaned forward, brought his face closer to hers. "Kiss me, Celeste."

She looked at that sexy mouth, thought of how many times she'd dreamed of kissing him, of tasting him, of exactly how it'd be to tease that sexy smirk with her tongue. Then she eased closer and made her dreams a reality.

The first touch of her mouth on his caused her entire body to shudder with need, a need to continue, to delve deeper for more. She swept her tongue against his lower lip and moaned her contentment when his mouth opened for her perusal. Easing her tongue inside, she couldn't control the urge to slowly slide her entire body against his as she tasted him. She yanked his shirt out of his jeans, hurriedly undid the remaining buttons and pushed the sides apart. Then she pressed her breasts against his chest, felt the rumbling beat of his heart against them, and was even more excited. She moved her tongue farther inside, stroking his, while her hips moved in direct correlation. Her need grew exponentially.

Dax's tongue mated with hers, then moved hungrily within her lips. He stroked the top of her mouth, slid over her teeth, then sucked her tongue. Her body began shivering, shaking. She'd never kissed anyone like this. She'd never been kissed like this.

The bulge between his legs grew even harder as she rubbed against it. She wanted him. And she didn't want to wait.

A low, deep growl rumbled from his throat and vibrated erotically against her tongue and mouth. That growl sent her desire higher still, knowing that Dax was on the edge as well, and she felt the burning inside getting stronger, hotter, pulling her deeper...pulling her...away.

No! her mind screamed when she realized what was happening. *No!*

"CELESTE!" Dax knew what had happened, but he couldn't believe that the powers that be would do that to him, to *them*. "Damn!"

She'd vanished, in the same way he'd seen ghosts fade away before, but none of their disappearances had ripped his heart out in their wake. One moment she'd been here, touching him, kissing him, driving him near mad with desire, and then—gone. And he was left hard, aching and ready. Ready for something that would possibly never happen. Had that been their last chance? Had she crossed over completely this time? And how would he know?

Just the thought of her hands on him, of her mouth on his, had his cock pressing solidly against his jeans. "Damn." He wanted her, and there was more to it than the physical need that had him hurting; he wanted Celeste, the woman who'd touched his heart in the summer when she stayed behind to help Chloe, and the one who, when she returned, had helped another young ghost before allowing her own needs to be sated. And she did have needs—intense needs.

"I've been with a boy, but I've never been with a man."

Well, she was sure as hell with a man tonight, but not nearly as intimately as Dax would have liked. Would they be given another chance?

Hell, both of them had helped Prissy first, in spite of the fact that they'd been two months without seeing each other, and without knowing if they'd ever see each other again, and the powers that be evidently hadn't taken *that* into consideration before they'd pulled her away—again.

The front door of the plantation slammed, and he jerked toward the sound. He couldn't control a swift surge of adrenaline at the possibility that Celeste had returned. But if she had come back, she wouldn't be using the door. "Who is it?"

"Dax?" Nanette called, then he listened to her footsteps as she headed up the stairs.

He buttoned his shirt, not bothering to tuck it in, since his hard-on was going to take some time to give up the ghost. Literally. "In here."

"Well, is she here?" Nan asked, entering the sitting room and looking around as though expecting to see someone with him.

"Who?" How would she know about Celeste?

"Your little ghost," she said, crossing the room and dropping into Adeline Vicknair's bentwood rocker. "Wait, I'm not sitting on her, right?"

"No," he said, still not quite believing how close he'd been to finally making love to Celeste only seconds ago. "She's with her parents, and for the record, Celeste isn't here either, though she was."

Nan's green eyes widened. "Celeste? She came back? How? When? She crossed, didn't she?"

"No, she didn't, and she came back with my ghost." He swallowed thickly. "And now she's gone again. Only I have no idea where she went. She was here until a few seconds ago, when the powers that be decided, without any forewarning whatsoever, that it was time for them to take her back."

She frowned. "Oh, Dax, I'm sorry. I know how much you wanted to be with her again." Nan tucked her legs beneath her. "So, she *hasn't* crossed?"

"She *hadn't* crossed," he clarified. "I have no idea if she crossed tonight or not."

"Surely not," she said, as though completely certain of the fact.

"What makes you say that?" Granted, he wanted to hear that Celeste was still hovering between the two sides, because obviously that meant he might get to see her again. But how could Nanette be so sure?

"Well, if she didn't cross before, with Chloe—that was the little girl she stayed behind for, right?"

"Right."

"Then why would she cross now? I mean, it must be something else that's keeping her in the middle. Something other than helping another spirit through."

"Part of me feels like I didn't cross because I couldn't leave you."

Dax really wanted to believe that was it, that she could control her destiny merely by wanting to be with him, but something told him there was more to it than that. And in order to help her stay on this side longer, maybe even permanently, he had to figure out what it was.

"How did she seem?" Nanette asked. "I mean, is she the same way Ryan was, where he chose to stay in the middle because he didn't want to cross? If memory serves, he rather liked it in the middle." She giggled. "Leave it to Monique to convince him that he'd rather satisfy one woman for life than tons of them in their dreams."

Dax blinked, and thought about what she'd said. "Ryan *did* control whether he crossed or not, didn't he?"

"That's what he said."

"I'm going to take a ride to Monique and Ryan's new place. I need to talk to my new brother-in-law." Dax stood from the settee.

Nan nodded, understanding dawning. "You think he can tell you how to keep her on this side."

"Well, if anyone can, it's him, and if there's any way possible, I *am* going to get her back."

Dax could feel his blood stir. Ryan had stayed. He'd been a ghost in the middle for over a year when he was assigned to Monique. Now he was living and breathing…and married to Dax's sister. Surely Ryan would know what was happening with Celeste, and how Dax could get her back to stay.

"He might not have all of the answers, but he'd sure have more than the two of us," she agreed. "He's lived in the middle, after all. When are you going to see him?"

"Right now."

"Well, tell me what you find out in the morning. I've got to get some sleep if I'm going to tackle all those ninth-graders first period. And they probably won't be all that thrilled to see me after I gave them that history assignment." She grinned. "Hey, I don't suppose you had a chance to look up any more information about *our* history tonight, did you?"

Dax shook his head. "Afraid not. From the time you left until just a few moments ago, I was fairly busy helping one ghost find the light...and trying to keep another one from even going near it."

"No problem," she said. "There's always tomorrow."

"You do realize that I work tomorrow, too," he said, "and that I'm somewhat preoccupied with getting Celeste back."

"Shoot, you're a pro at multitasking—keeping up your work, helping with the house, getting ghosts to the other side. And if there's a way, I'm betting you'll get Celeste back too. Face it, you always get the job done, no matter what the job is." Nan uncurled her legs from the chair and stood. "Why would this time be any different?"

She was right. Why shouldn't he be able to pull it all off this time? Only, this time he was talking about the ghost who'd controlled his entire being with her kiss.

"And Dax," she said as she started to walk away.

"Yeah?"

"Let me know when you get Celeste back."

"Don't worry, I'll let everyone know."

He left the house with Nanette's final words echoing in his thoughts. Nan hadn't said *if* you get Celeste back; she'd said *when*. And that was exactly how Dax felt. He'd lost her twice, but, on the reverse side of that, she'd made it to him twice too. If she could make it twice, she could make it again.

Third time, he prayed, was the charm. And hopefully, Ryan would offer a little insight about how to make it happen.

5

THE DRIVE FROM the plantation to Ormond, where Ryan and Monique's house was located, typically took about thirty minutes. Dax made it in twenty. He pulled onto their street and immediately noticed that the small house they were renting was lit up like an airport runway, with Ryan's truck piled high with furniture and backed up to the front door.

Dax parked the car and climbed out, immediately noticing that Tristan was here; his Jeep was parked outside. Obviously, Monique had recruited the oldest male cousin of the bunch to help unload, since her brothers were both preoccupied with hospital duty and helping spirits. Dax could only imagine the cussing Tristan was doing at being the only Vicknair here.

As if on cue, Tristan's tall frame exited the open front door of the house and he swore a stream of expletives that would make a sailor blush. "Did you leave *anything* at the plantation?" he asked sarcastically.

"Oh, stop complaining," Monique said, dusting her palms together as she followed him out. "This is the last load, and I've cut your hair for free since I opened my shop. You owe me."

"Shit, I'd rather pay for the cut." Tristan tested the weight of a tall dresser by lifting one end. "Tell your husband to get out here and help me with this one," he said, then apparently noticed Dax. "Scratch that, Dax is here. Come on over here. It's about time you showed up."

Monique brushed a big blond curl out of her eyes. "Hey, did you come to help?" she asked, then frowned. "You look terrible. What's up? Something wrong?"

"Yeah," Dax said. "Something is definitely wrong." A major understatement. He'd lost the woman he loved—twice.

"What happened?" she asked.

"Celeste. She came back, and then she left again." Dax helped Tristan maneuver the dresser off.

"Celeste? She came back?" Monique sounded as surprised as Dax had been when he'd first seen Celeste and Prissy in the sitting room. "Your ghost?"

His ghost. That was a nice way to think of her, but it was kind of hard to call Celeste "his" when he didn't know if he'd ever see her again. "Yeah, she came back today with my assigned spirit, and then she left."

"Left? As in, back to the other side?" Tristan asked.

"As in," Dax said, nodding. "And I've got to figure out how to get her back."

Tristan put his end of the dresser on the ground with a thud. "Come again?"

"I'm going to figure out how to bring her back, and I need Ryan to help me make that happen."

"That's my brother," Monique said, beaming. "Just because she's a ghost doesn't mean it can't work out."

Tristan shook his head. "Hell, the whole family's going nuts. First you go and marry a spirit, and now he's thinking he can bring back one who's crossed."

"I don't know if she's crossed or not," Dax explained. "My gut tells me she's stuck somewhere in the middle."

"You do realize it'd be a whole lot easier to find you a girl that's still breathing, don't you?" Tristan said, giving Dax one of his trademark skeptical looks that made most folks think twice about whatever they were contemplating.

Lucky for Dax, he was immune to it. "Hey, if I want your opinion, I'll ask for it." Typically, Tristan wouldn't have let that go without another smart-ass remark, but evidently, he could tell by Dax's tone that he wasn't in the mood to be messed with tonight, especially not when it came to Celeste.

"Like I said," Tristan repeated, "this family's losing it."

Monique moved to one end of the dresser. "I'll help Tristan with this. Why don't you head on into the kitchen. Ryan just carried some chairs in there, so you'll have a place to sit and talk. He's due a break anyway, he's been unloading trucks all day. And you don't need to worry about helping us, we're almost done. You concentrate on getting Celeste back."

Tristan's jaw fell. "You've gotta be kidding. You're

going to let him show up now, at the end of the day, and during the last load, and get by without helping? Shit, I'm just your cousin, he's your brother. I'd say he pulls rank on helping you move."

"I'm sorry, Tristan," Monique said sweetly. "Are your muscles hurting? I guess I assumed firemen were strong enough to take the heat."

"Hell," Tristan said, but he chuckled, and lifted his end.

"Now go talk to Ryan. Maybe he can help you figure out how to get her back," Monique instructed, ever the bossy sister. "Ryan! Dax is here, and he wants to talk to you. I'm sending him around." Moving slowly toward the house and grunting a little with each step, she glanced at Dax and ordered, "Walk around the side of the house," while Tristan backed through the front door and cussed when his knuckles scraped against the frame.

Following Monique's command, as if anybody in their right mind would tell her no, Dax rounded the house then climbed the steps leading to the kitchen, where Ryan was lifting a boxful of appliances onto the counter. His gray T-shirt had a sweat-dampened V from the neck to the chest, and his hair was even darker than usual, in wet waves from exertion.

"Come on in." He turned toward a red-and-white cooler shoved to one corner of the kitchen floor and withdrew two Cokes, then handed one to Dax. "Here. Monique said she didn't want us drinking beer while we're moving her furniture," he said with a shrug. "So, in the interest of maintaining marital bliss, this is the best I can do."

"Coke is fine," Dax said, taking the icy can from Ryan.

"Have a seat. I guess the two of us are supposed to take a break and chat, while Tristan busts his balls hauling furniture." He said the last words a little louder than the rest.

"I heard that," Tristan grumbled from the hall, and Monique laughed loudly.

Dax popped the top on the can, then took a much-needed dose of carbonated caffeine. He hadn't had a thing to eat or drink since that cup of coffee he'd had with Nan, not that he'd even thought of taking care of those types of physical needs while Celeste had been here. Taking care of sexual needs, on the other hand...

"So you need to talk to me?" Ryan asked, sitting at the table, then taking a long drink from his soda. "Damn, I'd really rather have a beer."

"Ryan?" Monique called sweetly, her voice echoing down the hallway from the front of the house.

"Yeah?"

"Honey, did you enjoy yourself last night?"

A long pause caused a noticeable silence.

"Did you?" she called again.

"Hell, yeah," Ryan finally answered.

"Well, if you want to enjoy tonight, you'll stop complaining about there being no beer in the house."

Another long pause, then Ryan shrugged, and smiled. "Deal."

"Good then, that's settled," she said rather triumphantly, either because she was getting her way now, or because she'd also be getting her way later.

Still grinning, Ryan asked, "Okay, what'd you want to ask me?"

"I want to know how you controlled where you went when you were in the middle. Or rather, when you visited someone who was living."

Ryan placed his drink on the table and leaned back in his chair. "How I controlled it?"

"Yeah. How did you go back and forth, from the middle to this side? What did you do to make it happen?"

Ryan's head shook slightly as he answered. "I didn't do anything. I thought about where I wanted to go, or who I wanted to see, and I went. That's all there was to it."

"You're saying you just had to think about it?" Dax asked, baffled. Why had Ryan been able to act like any other ghost when Celeste couldn't?

"I had total control over it." Ryan folded his arms at his chest. "Why are you asking?"

"It's Celeste. She came back today, and we were together for a little while, not nearly long enough, and then she was pulled away again." Dax didn't bother explaining who Celeste was; Ryan knew her from his time in the middle. In fact, when Ryan had been hovering between the other side and the living, Monique had tried to play matchmaker between the two spirits, but Ryan had already fallen for Monique. However, they *were* friends, which meant Ryan understood her, and not only that, he understood her current situation, living in the middle.

"I thought Celeste crossed over with Chloe," Ryan said.

"I thought so too, but she didn't, and she came back today to help another little girl cross, and…"

"And?" Ryan asked.

"And to be with me."

Ryan nodded, not needing further information. He obviously remembered what it was like to be caught between this side and the light, and he'd know more than anyone how hard it was when the one you loved wasn't dwelling on the same side of the spectrum. "I don't know why she wouldn't be able to come and go at will. It doesn't make sense."

"You never knew of ghosts who would get—stuck—in either place, or something like that?"

"I'm sorry, man, but no," he said. "Are you saying that she didn't seem to have any control over when she left you today? She couldn't have maybe thought of another place, or someone else, and gone to them? Maybe a family member or something? I mean, that would happen to me—if I got something on my mind, I'd simply go there, wherever it was."

"She didn't have any control over it. I'm sure of that," Dax said. "And trust me, she wasn't thinking about any other place, or any other person, at the time." She'd been thinking of him, only him, and the fact that they were finally together, the same way he'd been thinking of her.

Ryan took another sip of his drink, then closed his eyes and leaned his head back. After a couple of seconds, he sat forward and looked at Dax. "She hasn't been given to anyone else as an assignment, has she? I mean, a medium to help her cross?"

"None of the Vicknair mediums," Dax said. "We're certainly not the only folks helping ghosts find their way through, but I think she'd have mentioned it."

"Yeah, you're probably right. Plus, more than likely she'd come to one of you, since she's been to the Vicknair place twice already, don't you think?"

Dax nodded.

"Okay. So she can't control when she comes to this side. Did she say where she goes when she isn't with you?"

"She said she didn't know."

Ryan frowned, shook his head. "Hell, man, I don't know either. I mean, my experience was totally different. I saw the light but didn't want to go through, and then, later on, the powers that be wouldn't let me. In my case, it was because I needed to learn how to love."

"And thank goodness you figured out how," Monique chimed in from the doorway.

Ryan smiled, but Dax didn't.

"So you don't know what I can do to help her get back through?" he asked, feeling defeated.

His brother-in-law's grin disappeared, and he looked solemnly toward Dax. "I wish I did, but if she can't move freely within the middle, then I don't know what to tell you. That's nothing like what I went through, and, truthfully, I can't figure out why she hasn't crossed over."

"*If* she hasn't," Dax said. What was to say that she

hadn't crossed tonight, after the two of them had shared that phenomenal kiss?

"Oh, Dax." Monique entered the kitchen with Tristan close at her heels. She wrapped an arm around him consolingly.

Dax shrugged to shake off her arm. He didn't want consolation; he wanted answers. "What about sleeping?" he asked. "Have you ever known of ghosts who got tired when they came to this side?"

"Tired?" Ryan repeated. "Ghosts don't get tired, Dax. Why would they?"

"She did. And I don't mean a little sleepy either, I mean exhausted, nearly-ready-to-pass-out tired. I saw her like that today, twice."

"A ghost? Tired?" Tristan repeated from the doorway. "I've never seen it."

"Me, neither," said Monique.

"Well, trust me, she was," Dax said.

"That's not—well, it's not normal," Tristan said. "Seriously, why would they need sleep?"

"I don't know," Dax admitted. "But there were other things about her that were different too," he thought aloud.

"Like what?" Monique moved to sit in Ryan's lap, while Tristan grabbed a Coke from the cooler and joined them at the table.

"Yeah, what else?" Tristan asked. "Maybe we can help you figure out what's going on."

"Her clothes. Last time she was here, she was always

in the same thing, a yellow tank top and jeans. I assumed that's what she was wearing when she died."

"But that wasn't what she wore this time?" Monique asked.

"No. She wore a white gown."

"Like a wedding gown?" Tristan asked, surprise evident in his tone.

"No, *not* like a wedding gown," Dax said, growing irritated but still wanting answers. "A nightgown, a long, satin nightgown." A very sexy nightgown that barely balanced on her shoulders and looked as though if he could only ease it down the smoothness of her arms, it would puddle to the ground.

Dax's imagination was way too vivid, and the image of Celeste, standing beautifully nude before him, was crystal clear. Would the real thing be better than the fantasy? Oh, yeah, he knew it would. But would he ever see her that way? Would he ever see her again at all?

"You changed clothes in the middle," Monique said to Ryan, and he nodded.

"Yeah, I did."

"How?" Dax asked, realizing he needed to pay attention to any insight Ryan could offer.

"The same way I moved from one place to another. I thought about what I wanted to wear, and my clothing changed."

"Just like that?" Dax asked.

Ryan nodded. "Pretty much. Really, there wasn't anything to it. I thought about it, and I changed."

"I remember you went from jeans and a T-shirt to a tuxedo right in front of me," Monique said, and her husband smiled.

"Yeah, I remember that night."

Dax shook his head. None of this was adding up. "But you changed clothes based on where you were going, what you were doing or who you were seeing, right? I mean, you picked clothing to go with whatever you had going on, didn't you?"

"Yeah," Ryan agreed.

"Celeste came with Prissy and went with her to the hospital, and then she spent time with me back at the house. And the whole time she wore that same gown. Don't you think that if she could control what she was wearing, she'd have picked something different than a nightgown? And it wasn't because she died in it, because she obviously died in that jeans and tank top that she wore last time."

"Maybe it was because she knew she was going to be sleeping while she was here," Tristan said with a smirk, then held up his palms when Dax glared at him. "Hey, I worked all day and hauled furniture all night, forgive me if I'm leaning toward sarcasm."

Monique twisted in Ryan's lap. "Honey, do you remember anything from being in the middle that would help Dax figure out what's causing her to be so different from all our other spirits?"

Again, Ryan shook his head. "If I did, I'd tell you."

"Anything else out of the ordinary with her?" she

asked. "Something that might help us figure out why she's stuck in the middle? Other than the sleeping and the clothing, was there anything else different from other ghosts? Did she glow like our regular spirits?"

Dax started to nod, but then he thought about Celeste and Prissy, standing side by side in the sitting room. The little girl's body had been cloaked in a brilliant, golden glow, so bright that Dax had nearly had to squint to look at her. But Celeste's appearance hadn't been nearly as bright.

"No," he said. "No, she didn't. Her body was illuminated, but it wasn't as vivid as the younger spirit's. But—"

"But?" Monique prompted.

"But when she got tired, and then again, right before she left, her body glowed brighter, not quite as bright as my usual spirits, but it was more gold than white."

Ryan cleared his throat. "I don't know about the other things that are different, but that one does have a reasonable answer, based on what I remember about the middle."

"What is it?" Dax asked.

"When I saw other spirits getting closer to the light, they always glowed brighter. I assumed that the closer a spirit was to crossing, the brighter their essence became."

Dax closed his eyes and pictured Celeste, getting brighter and brighter, right until she left. That *did* make sense, and he knew why he hadn't thought of it on his own. Subconsciously, he hadn't wanted to face the fact that touching him, kissing him, might have made it harder for her to fight the pull of the light. What if being with him today had *forced* her to cross? "Damn."

"Hey, man, I'm not saying she crossed over. I'm merely saying that when ghosts glow brighter, that usually means that they're closer to the other side. She could still be in the middle. I fought crossing, remember? And if she wants to be with you the way I wanted to be with Monique, she's fighting it too."

Dax swallowed, nodded. Celeste would fight it; he had no doubt. But she'd been weak today. "Thanks," he said, standing. He needed to go back to the plantation and think, try to put the pieces together and figure out where Celeste was, and how to help her get where she needed to be—on this side, with him.

"I'm not sure why you're thanking us. I don't think we were all that much help." Tristan finished off his soda then tossed the can in the trash.

"Talking through things always helps," Dax said, knowing that they had, in fact, given him more to think about. Celeste was getting pulled toward the light, and he didn't want to give the other side the advantage by making her weaker. But he did want her here, and to feel her body, her mouth, her *everything* against him again. "I'm going home."

Then he remembered the boxes in Ryan's truck. "Hell, I'm being a louse. I'll help you finish unloading first."

Tristan smirked. "We're finished, and I was blowing off steam anyway. It wasn't that much stuff, and I didn't mind helping. I just like to complain."

"Now, *that's* the truth," Monique said. "I haven't given you a haircut yet that you didn't find something wrong with."

"Watch it," Tristan warned, "or I'll take my business elsewhere."

"As if you could find someone else to cut it for free." Climbing out of Ryan's lap, she took Dax's arm and led him down the hall to the front of the house. When the two of them were out of earshot of Ryan and Tristan, she lowered her voice and asked, "Are you going to be okay?"

"Yeah. Just got to figure out what's going on, somehow," he said.

"I wish we could be more help. If Ryan thinks of anything else that might help you figure out what's happening with her, I'll call you, okay?" She looked past Dax to the back of Ryan's truck, the tailgate opened to lie flush against the porch. "I'm really glad that was the last load. We've been hauling and unloading all day. And now I get to start unpacking it all."

Dax surveyed the boxes and furniture stacked in the foyer, in the dining room and down the hall. "I didn't realize you had this much stuff, sis."

"I didn't, but there's tons of furniture in the attic at the plantation, and Nanette told me I might as well take some of it. I didn't even realize she'd been going up there and covering it all in plastic to protect it from the storms. Or she did until we got the roof fixed."

"Nanette cares a lot about saving the old stuff, the furniture *and* the house," he said.

"As if you don't care just as much. I don't know what the rest of us would do without you two urging us on. And I'm glad you haven't moved out of the plantation—I'd have felt a bit guilty leaving if I thought Nan was going to be living there and trying to keep that big place up alone."

"I love that place," Dax said honestly. Truthfully, he'd never considered living anywhere else. Even when he went to LSU in Baton Rouge, he'd commuted, because he didn't want to be that far from the house that meant so much to him. Nanette was right; the plantation was their legacy, and he planned to help her keep it that way, both by restoring it with the rest of the family and by finding proof that it was inhabited during the Civil War.

"Whoa, where'd your mind go?" she asked.

"Thinking about the house."

"Well, you should check out all the neat things up in the attic sometime. Most of it is still in plastic, but it's in great shape, particularly for stuff so old." She smiled. "I'm kind of excited about having furniture that belonged to our ancestors in mine and Ryan's house. It's nice to be able to give things a second chance to live, you know?"

"Yeah, it is," Dax agreed, but he wasn't referring to old furniture. And he still had to figure out how to give Celeste *her* second chance.

6

CELESTE HAD NEVER had such a difficult time getting back to the middle. She stumbled, fell down, then used a wall for leverage to stand up again. She had to keep moving, had to get away from the cries behind her, and back to Dax. She'd found her way through with Prissy, with Adeline Vicknair's help. She'd simply get back to the middle and ask Adeline to let her through again, and this time she'd beg the older woman to let her stay—at least long enough to make love with Dax just once, if she couldn't be with him forever.

With every ounce of her strength, she edged forward. She knew that the center room was near; a faint glow illuminated the pathway ahead, and she had no doubt that the glimmering was from its light. Was another spirit going through now? Or was a child there needing help? Both times when Celeste had helped children, she'd been able to see Dax. Maybe that's why the light was there; another child was waiting and needing her help—needing *their* help.

She finally reached the opening to the middle room, but was dismayed to see no other spirit in its center. She was completely alone, yet the light was steadily growing brighter, the same way it had when Cassie passed through. As always, Celeste felt drawn to its warmth, drawn to its unique allure. She was so cold, and she knew that merely getting nearer to that potent beam would warm her all over.

She wanted to be warm again.

Celeste didn't want to pass through, she had to get back to Dax, but she did want to get warm. She stepped toward the light, leaned her head back and let the powerful glow wash over her from head to toe. It felt so good, so perfect. She took another step forward and knew before she looked that the opening had expanded. The blissful heat claimed the entire room now, warming her from the inside out, and her pains started to fade. She could feel her exhaustion lifting, and nothing but freedom from her burdens waiting on the other side.

No more exhaustion, no more pain.

Another step forward...

Cries. Wails. Her name. All of those sounds echoed from the hallway to her right, the path she'd just come down. Why couldn't she remember what was at the end of that path?

"Celeste!" they yelled. "Please! No!"

She swallowed, backed away from the powerfully tempting radiance, and immediately her exhaustion returned. The light had grown to nearly the size of a door, but now it started shrinking away, like golden water down a drain.

Celeste fell to the floor. She knew those voices wanted her to go to them, but she didn't want to. And now that the light had disappeared again, she wasn't tempted to go in that direction either. She turned to her left, saw the edge of the path that led to Dax and crawled toward it. "Please," she whispered, then licked her parched lips. "Adeline, please, let me through."

Nothing happened.

Sobs tore from her chest, echoed against the roof of the dismal room and then came back to haunt her. "Please," she pleaded, her body collapsing against the cold floor. She was *not* going back down the other path until she saw him. She wouldn't. "Let—me—in!"

"Oh, darling, what have I done? You've barely rested, *chère*."

Celeste knew the owner of the voice. Adeline Vicknair had, once again, opened the pathway to Dax. Merely seeing the older woman, and knowing she had the power to send her back to Dax, gave Celeste a surge of much-needed strength.

She sat up, then pushed to her feet. "I've got to see him again, Adeline. I've got to get back to him."

"*Chère*, you only left a few hours ago. If I let you back through, you won't be able to stay any time at all. You're simply too weak, child. You need to rest, and then, maybe, you can try again."

"I'm going now, and you're going to help me," Celeste said, with conviction. "I *won't* rest until I do."

"But you see, dear, you have a choice to make. Either

that way—" she pointed to the middle, where the light had been blazing merely seconds ago "—or that one." Adeline indicated the path to the right, where the voices still called Celeste's name. "Dax's path can't be your final destination. It isn't an option, and every time you go to him, you risk losing the ability to choose. I know you want to see him, and I'm trying to help you."

"Then do. Let me through, Adeline. Help me," she whispered.

Adeline's mouth flattened, then she closed her eyes as though deciding what to do.

"Please," Celeste urged.

"On one condition."

"Anything."

The older woman stepped back and pushed the door wide, then she lowered her voice to a hushed whisper. "Promise me, *chère*, that you won't tempt fate. Promise me that you won't push yourself until you're too tired to fight the light's pull. If that happens, you *will* lose your ability to choose."

"I promise," Celeste said, though she wasn't completely certain she could keep that vow. How would she know when she'd stayed too long? She was tired the last time she was taken from him, but she didn't enter the light. Surely she could keep it from happening again. She simply had to resist, be strong—strong for Dax. He was definitely worth the fight.

Besides, she wasn't concerned with having choices

right now; in her mind there was only one choice to make, and she was making it.

FOR DAX sleep was both an enemy and a friend. An enemy, because it took time away from his quest to get Celeste back, but a friend, because every time he closed his eyes, he found her in his dreams. And although he knew that that was what was happening now, that the dream had taken over, he didn't care. Instead, he focused on making it as real as possible, so much that he could almost—almost— feel her presence nearby the bed. But ultimately he couldn't deny that this was a dream; in reality, he'd never seen Celeste nude. But he saw her that way now.

Dax had known she would be beautiful beneath the white gown, but *beautiful* was too weak a word for what he was envisioning now.

She was exquisite.

Long, golden curls tumbled freely past her shoulders, teasing the tips of her breasts. She stood before him, her skin satin smooth and glowing faintly, as he took his time appreciating her beauty, imprinting her image on his thoughts to hold on to for eternity.

He never wanted to forget this moment. He never wanted to forget *her*. "Move your hair," he said. "Please, I want to see you, Celeste, all of you."

With a soft, seductive smile, she pushed her long curls behind her shoulders, and his jaw clenched tight. Her breasts were fuller than he'd anticipated, high and taut and beautifully exposed, the tips hard points that he longed to lick, taste, suck. Her waist was slim and gently flared outward to curved hips and well-toned legs. Between those legs, soft, blond curls covered her most tender flesh, and Dax grew painfully hard merely looking at her and imagining touching her there, kissing her there, coming inside of her *there*.

"I need you, Celeste." His words were rough, strained and commanding. "I've waited for this for too long, and I don't want to wait any longer." He watched her step closer to his bed. "How long do we have?"

Her touch on his wrist caught him by surprise. He hadn't realized she was that close, and he hadn't seen her reach for him, but she was definitely touching him now, the searing sensation that he'd experienced earlier, the first time she'd touched him, heating his body like a brushfire, causing him to groan in near pain, in near ecstasy.

He tried to reach for her, but his arm didn't move. "Celeste?" His brain told him this wasn't really happening; it couldn't be. She was still gone, still somewhere in the middle, in a place he couldn't go, but this dream seemed so real that he didn't want it to end, not before he had her, if only in his mind.

He refused to open his eyes, refused to let reality in, but still her image was fading. Something was taking the vision away, and he suspected he knew what that something was, or rather who. Hell, he didn't like following their rules, but he did, every time. And now that *he* needed something, needed Celeste, the powers that be weren't even willing to give him a damn fantasy?

No! Dammit, don't take this too!

Her searing touch moved to his other wrist, and he felt his arm being pulled above his head. Heat, once again, spread over him, and he could feel sweat beading from his pores. More than mere warmth, the lust, the pent-up desire, sizzled throughout his flesh, and Dax could no longer keep from verifying what he now suspected.

This wasn't a dream.

He opened his eyes and saw the woman currently binding his wrist to the bedpost, long spirals of hair cascading around her shoulders the same way that they had in his dream. She wasn't nude anymore, proof enough that he wasn't dreaming. Instead, she wore the long, white gown, and her face was intent on what she was doing, securing him to the bed. His arms were stretched in a V and fastened to each of the bedposts. She was here, with him, and she'd tied his hands in preparation for…everything. "I'm not dreaming."

"No, you aren't," she said, knotting one of his silk neckties around his wrist as she spoke. She finished, then turned toward him. "You were dreaming of me," she said with a smile, and her silver-gray eyes glittered as she spoke.

"I've dreamed of you every night for the past two months," he said. "But this time, it was so real, even before you touched me."

"Dax, I—I know I won't have long this time. I was supposed to rest before I came, but I couldn't stay away. I needed more."

He knew exactly what she meant. "I know. I need more too. I need you, Celeste."

She swallowed. "I want to touch you again, and to kiss you again, but—"

"But?" he asked, and he prayed that she wasn't going to say that she wouldn't touch him this time. He needed her touch, ached for it, didn't know if he'd keep breathing without it. His skin still tingled from where she'd bound his wrists, and he wanted to burn like that everywhere. And he suspected that the same exhilarating near-orgasmic feeling that he experienced every time she touched him was reciprocated. He could tell by the way her skin instantly flushed when she touched him, by the way her eyes grew darker, more intense, filled with need.

"But I know now that every time I touch you, I'll grow weaker, and while I don't plan to let that stop me, I want you to know that if I'm pulled away again, that's why."

He focused on her words, and wrapped his brain around the biggest problem they were facing. "So that *is* what makes you leave," he stated. "Touching me."

"Growing weak makes me leave, and interacting with someone who is living makes me weak." She smiled almost playfully. "But I want to interact with you, Dax, as closely as I possibly can."

He smiled as well, but continued to try to figure out how they could make the most of their time together. He wanted her, there was no denying that, and he really didn't want to wait to make it happen. But if touching him made her leave quicker…

"Hell, this is going to be tough, but I want you here, for as long as you can stay." He took a deep breath, thought about her hands caressing him, igniting him, burning. "How do you feel now?"

She brought her mouth close to his. "Excited."

He laughed. "You're not going to make this easy."

"Make what easy?" she asked, and he could swear she was inhaling his scent as she spoke. But that wasn't possible. Or it shouldn't be. Ghosts shouldn't inhale anything, but then again, ghosts shouldn't sleep, either.

"My proposition. That we talk for a while first, before you touch me, and before you grow weaker."

"That's probably still considered interacting with someone who's living, don't you think?" she asked, and her eyes grew darker still as she tenderly put her tongue against his lower lip, then slid it inside.

Dax couldn't stop her. And hell, he didn't want to. He opened his mouth and accepted the sweet taste of her, sizzling and even more intense than the touches on his wrists. There was a living flame within her, hotter than anything he'd ever experienced with a breathing woman, and he couldn't get enough. His tongue joined hers and they stroked against each other as she moved on top of him, the satin fabric of her gown and his thin sheet the only obstacles between her body and his.

Her gown. Memories of his conversation with Ryan invaded the moment, bringing with it the realization that he needed to try to control the sexual intensity of this, or she'd disappear again, and he'd have wasted a chance to find out how to hold on to this, hold on to her, for longer than a mere visit.

It took every ounce of willpower to break away from her kiss. "Celeste. Please."

"Anything," she whispered. "Just tell me what to do. I want to learn."

Have mercy, she was going to be the death of him. "Trust me, you're doing fine," he said, then pulled against his restraints to move his head up on the pillow. She hadn't bound him overly tight, and he suspected that if he pulled hard enough, both hands would be free. But hell, that'd really get him in hot water with the powers that be, wouldn't it? And they had let her come back, even if only briefly, so he didn't want to do anything to piss them off.

"Then what is it?" she asked, and Dax noticed the concern in her eyes. "Dax, I know I'll get pulled away again, and I have no idea when that will happen. I don't want to waste time."

"Neither do I, believe me. But I also don't want to lose you again without trying to figure out how to get you back. I know there's got to be a way, and I'm thinking you can help me figure it out if we talk for a minute." He smiled at her, and eased his body to the side so he couldn't feel her through the sheet. He needed to make this last, and weakening her wasn't the way to make that happen. ⌐e⌐ s talk a little first."

The pain in her eyes touched his heart. "Dax, if I cross without ever making love to you, I'll never forgive myself for not taking advantage of this chance."

He wanted to ask her so many questions—why she couldn't control the time she came to him or the time she left, why she grew tired when no other ghost he'd ever known needed sleep, why she was wearing that night-gown again, if indeed she could change her clothes at will. And if she couldn't change, then why couldn't she, when Ryan had been able to? So many questions, but looking into her eyes, he realized—none of them mattered. What if they started talking, as he'd suggested, and then she was pulled away before they touched again? Could he forgive himself if he caused her to cross, completely, and never experienced making love with her?

"I don't want to talk either," he said honestly. "I want you, Celeste."

She smiled and stood from the bed. Then she looked at him, and her gray eyes turned charcoal with desire. "In your dream, what was I wearing?"

"Nothing."

She moved one finger to her shoulder and pushed the shiny fabric down, then she shifted slightly, and the other side also spilled down her arm, so the fabric rested at her elbows, and her breasts were bare.

His dream had been amazingly accurate. Full and lush and tipped with rose-tinted peaks, they were perfect. As in his dream, he ached to caress them with his mouth, and to learn the sweet sounds she'd make when he did. He wanted to learn what excited her, what aroused her, what ignited that slow burn within her until it exploded…around him.

She shifted her hips slightly and dropped her arms to her sides, and the fabric continued on its path to the floor.

Dax's erection pushed high against the sheet, and he forced himself to breathe. She was naked, boldly, beautifully naked, and exceptional, from the tiny navel that centered her slim waist, to the curved hips, a little more than in his dream, and damn if he didn't like the extra too. Her legs, as he'd imagined, were toned and well sculpted, perfect for nuzzling when they finally made love, and he would nuzzle them, kiss them, caress them, on his path to her core, hidden from his view with shimmering golden curls. He wanted to part those curls and taste her, feel the most heated part of her against his tongue, feel her pulse against his mouth as she came.

She turned toward the bed and he watched her attention move to the tented portion of the sheet, and the damp spot where he was already preparing to enter her. "You said it has been a long time," she whispered, then her hands grasped the sheet, and she slowly slid it down his body, eyeing each revealed inch of his flesh. "How long has it been?"

Her eyes were nearly black as she looked up at him from the foot of the bed. In the back of his mind, he knew that something wasn't right about that either. Her eyes had been lighter earlier, then darker, and now darker still. But he didn't have time to analyze it, because she dropped the sheet to the floor, then climbed up on the bed, and took his breath away. Her hair fell wildly across his legs as she brought her face near his erection and asked again, "How long has it been, Dax?"

"I haven't been with a woman since I met you," he said, giving her the truth. "No one else would do."

Her hands circled his penis, and then she brought her mouth to the tip and licked the first drops away.

The heat of Celeste's mouth was even more potent, as though he were being flicked with hot coal…and he didn't ever want it to stop. He'd never had any sexual encounter remotely like this, where he honestly felt as if his body couldn't take it, but he prayed that it could.

"I've never done this before, Dax, and yet, I can sense exactly how this makes you feel, exactly where you want me to touch, exactly what you want me to do. It's—it's making me burn inside."

Dax grit his teeth and nodded, unable to speak. He didn't want to lose control, not yet, but the heat was so intense that he knew he wouldn't make it much longer. He wrapped his hands tighter within their restraints and forced himself to leave them where they were. He couldn't touch her, but he wanted to, to reach down and take that exquisite mouth and pull it to his, then slide her hips up his body and learn if she was as hot there.

She was trembling all over, her body shaking as she placed hot, wet kisses down his penis, massaging him with fiery circles of her tongue, until she reached the base. Then, emitting a low moan of contentment, she took that same technique to his testicles, and Dax's heartbeat soared, thundering in his chest, roaring in his ears. His pulse hammered through him, his need for release beckoning him to let go.

Celeste licked him solidly again, from base to tip, then she ran her tongue around the end and took him inside, deep inside, and another of her intense moans vibrated against his heated flesh as she worked her way up and down, up and down, moaning and clamping that hot mouth tighter against him, until Dax's body tensed fiercely, a tingling rush poured through him, and he growled through an orgasm that tore from his very soul.

He sucked in a breath, exhilarated by what she'd done for him, and miserable because he feared what it would cost her. She wanted to experience making love, but now that she'd put so much of her energy into pleasing him...

"Celeste!" he yelled as she looked up at him, her black eyes filled with pleasure at what she'd done, and no regrets, none at all. "Celeste!" he repeated, then he watched in complete agony as the woman he wanted more than any other—disappeared.

7

Dax was covered in sweat, both from the orgasm that had thoroughly shaken his world and from anger at losing Celeste again without fulfilling *her* needs, or learning how to get her back. "Dammit!"

He yanked his hands free from the restraints, then climbed from the bed and hurriedly dressed, grabbing the first clothing he could find, worn jeans and a black tank undershirt. The digital clock beside the bed proclaimed it two-thirty in the morning, but Dax didn't care what time it was; he needed answers, and he wasn't going to find them while he slept. More than that, he needed help, and he believed he knew where to go to get it.

Obviously, no one on this side was able to provide him with the help he needed. If anyone could have, it'd have been Ryan. But there was one person on the other side who had never let him down, and that person surely had the ability to help him now.

Even though he was only four when she passed on, he remembered one thing he could always count on from the feisty Vicknair matriarch. No matter how hard Adeline Vicknair tried, she simply couldn't tell him no.

Maybe it was because he was her youngest grandson. Maybe it was because he'd been as headstrong and trying back then as he was now. Or maybe it was just that all his older siblings, cousins, parents, aunts and uncles had spoiled him rotten. But for whatever reason, not once could he remember the woman turning him down, for anything.

Dax was counting on her not to break that record.

His bedroom was on the second floor of the plantation, so it was a short walk to the sitting room, its traditional rose-tinted lighting spilling from beneath the doorway across the hardwood in the hall.

One of the plantation's oddities that the Vicknairs had grown accustomed to over the years, Adeline's fringed antique lamp never burned out, not when the light was switched off, nor when the power in the entire parish was out due to storms, or even when the bulb was removed. As a matter of fact, even when Katrina took its toll, this room remained lit.

Tonight was no exception.

He pushed through the double doors and entered the undeniably feminine room, where big bold roses covered the wallpaper and shades of pink and burgundy covered nearly everything else, and he stormed toward the coffee table where the silver tea service sat, shining as it reflected the lamplight.

"I want answers, and I can't get them without your help," Dax said, dropping onto the settee and then leaning toward the silver platter. He stared at the open space between the ornate pitcher and two gleaming silver cups, the spot where Adeline sent all of their assignments. He'd never asked for anything beyond what she'd provided, or rather, he'd never asked for anything beyond what *they'd* provided. Never. He'd always taken his assignments as they came, used the information to help spirits cross, and never even considered asking for anything more.

But that was before Celeste. Before tonight.

"If I cross without ever making love to you, I'll never forgive myself for not taking advantage of this chance."

If the powers that be had sent her to the other side before she'd known what it felt like to be completely and thoroughly satisfied by a man, *to be completely and thoroughly satisfied by him,* he'd be damned before he'd ever help them again.

"I am *not* leaving this room until you give me something to work with here," he said. "I swear it, and you know damn well I mean it."

Two heavy heartbeats passed, then two more, before a thick sheet of lavender paper, the size of a postcard, appeared in the center of the silver tray with his name scrawled across the outside in his grandmother's script, but not nearly as neat as usual.

Good, he had her attention.

He snatched it up and turned it over, eager to see what she'd say. Her message was scribbled even more hastily than his name had been on the other side, and true to her nature, she didn't waste time getting to the point.

There is no need for cursing, young man. You may be twenty-three, but I'm still your grandmother, and believe it or not, I do have friends in very high places! Good God, and to think I actually believed Celeste was the more stubborn of you two.

Dax's tension eased a bit. So she thought Celeste was stubborn too. He'd have to agree about that, particularly after he'd attempted to get her to slow down and talk to him, and she'd outright refused to do anything less than what she wanted. Luckily for him, it happened to be pleasing him more than any other woman ever had.

Yes, his grandmother was right. Celeste was stubborn. Wild and sweet and tempting and adorable and sexy…and stubborn. Well, fine. Dax had a feeling it'd take two hardheaded and determined souls to get her back on this side, and obviously, between the two of them, they fit the bill.

He read the rest of his grandmother's note, written in sharp, slanted penmanship, as though she was in a hurry, or really pissed, or both. Dax wasn't overly concerned. She was helping him, and that was what he wanted. Plus, she was his grandmother, and she'd love him no matter how much he ticked her off.

Okay, first of all—she hasn't crossed, not yet anyway. Although if you keep exhausting her, she will, and there won't be a thing I can do about it. You can't continue to tempt fate, Dax.

Second, she needs to rest, and I'm making her stay here longer this time. Yes, I'll let her back through, when

I think she can make the trip, but don't expect to see her for at least a few days. And in the meantime, use the brains God gave you to figure out how to get her back. I am not allowed to tell you, Dax, so you're going to have to figure this one out on your own. But you are the puzzle solver of the bunch; use your talents to put the pieces together.

Third, and this is important, the only clue I can give you. What you need, and what Nanette needs too for that matter, is in the attic. That's all I can say.

One more thing, and I thought you knew already, but…the no-touching rule. It only applies to your hands, chère. It ONLY applies to your hands.

Dax gawked at the words on the page, absorbing all of the information before—

The note disappeared, and he struggled to mentally repeat the information she'd provided, so he wouldn't forget. Celeste hadn't crossed and she'd return, but he couldn't let her get exhausted or he'd lose her; they'd have to be more careful next time. He'd have to control the beyond-natural sexual urges they had for each other and force her to slow down, force himself to slow down too. He wanted her, but he was determined that next time he wouldn't be the only one to have an orgasm.

And he *could* touch her? Not with his hands, but hell, there were plenty of other body parts he could use, in plenty of interesting ways. If he'd only known earlier, he would most certainly have given her what she needed.

No use wasting time thinking about what he would

have done now. Next time, he'd do it all, repeatedly, but he'd have to find a way to spread their lovemaking out, to take their time and not let her drain her energy so quickly. A challenge for sure, but a challenge he was definitely up to. Keeping her here longer was worth it.

And speaking of a challenge, Adeline's note had given him a place to look for answers. The attic.

Dax left the sitting room and took the stairs two at a time to the third floor and the attic access. The string to open the attic door was typically wrapped around the door's tiny knob in the ceiling, well above nine feet high, but tonight it was hanging down and waiting for Dax's arrival.

He pulled on the string and the folding ladder came barreling straight at him like an arrow heading for a target. Dax jumped out of the way just in time to keep the thing from colliding with his head.

Looking down the hallway, he waited for Nanette to come check out the racket. Surely something as loud as that ladder pounding against the floor would wake her, but after a minute passed and there was still no sign of his oldest cousin, he climbed on up. Obviously, she was a sound sleeper. He swallowed, immediately thinking of Celeste sleeping in the hospital chair in Mr. Fontenot's room. Dax had tried to wake her when he first arrived, but he couldn't even make her stir. For a moment, he'd considered the possibility that she was dead, then had realized how foolish that was. She *was* dead. But she was also exhausted. And he still couldn't fathom how that was possible. But hopefully, he'd figure it out soon, with the help of something in this attic.

The light from the hallway below illuminated a small portion of the room, but Dax knew the only light within the massive attic was a single pull-string bulb. He waved his hands in front of him as he moved so he could find the string. It took several kicked boxes and even more knocks into furniture, but he finally found it, with his face. He moved his hand to the thin nylon, pulled it, and saw that in spite of Monique's haul, the place was still at least three-fourths full of furniture, boxes and plain old *stuff*.

"What I need is in the attic," he repeated from his grandmother's note. "Couldn't you give me something a little more vague?" he asked sarcastically.

A loud, roaring clap of thunder rattled the side of the house, and Dax knew this thunder didn't come from a storm. It hadn't rained in days, nor was it supposed to.

"Fine," he said, grinning in spite of his predicament. "I appreciate your help, Grandma Adeline, but really, don't you think it might be a bit difficult for me to figure out what it is I'm looking for?"

Another booming clap of thunder, louder than the first, provided his answer.

Dax scrubbed a hand down his face, remembered the golden-haired beauty that was worth whatever it took to bring her back for good and uncovered the closest piece of furniture, a tall highboy dresser. He opened each of the drawers, slid his hand inside to check for contents and found none.

What was he looking for, anyway?

"One down. A thousand to go."

He moved to a box nearby, rummaged through its contents and found a variety of antique kitchenware. Old-fashioned sifters, potato mashers and even aluminum Jell-O molds were stuffed inside. He moved to another box filled with crocheted doilies of various shapes and sizes, which brought back an early memory of his grandmother, crocheting in the Bentwood rocker in her sitting room. He dropped the doilies back in the box, then sat on the dusty floor and surveyed the eternity of furniture and boxes surrounding him. Wasn't that just his luck? He was the descendant of packrats, and finding whatever he was looking for in two centuries' worth of their accumulation could very well take him longer than he had, longer than Celeste had.

Kitchen gadgets and doilies. Dax couldn't imagine how any of those items were supposed to help him get Celeste back. Narrowing his search was necessary, but he had to determine how. Boxes were scattered sporadically throughout the room, some sitting solo, others stacked up four high. It'd take longer to go through them than the furniture, particularly if every box was packed with *dreegailles*, the Cajuns' popular term for junk.

Then again, one man's junk was another man's treasure. And his treasure, the answer to bringing Celeste back, was somewhere in this attic. He decided the best plan of action was to actually have a plan. There were way more boxes than pieces of furniture, so he decided to tackle the job according to ratio. He guessed three boxes for every one piece of furniture, so since he was already two boxes down, he grabbed another, and prepared for a long night.

After thirty minutes, he'd been through nine boxes mostly filled with ancient knickknacks and three pieces of empty furniture. So far, he'd discovered nothing that looked remotely useful. In fact, he hadn't found the first thing that even suggested his ancestors had ghosts visiting the plantation at all, which wasn't that odd, since the family did its best to protect their secret. But his grandmother had indicated that what he needed was here, and since what he needed would certainly have something to do with ghosts, he knew he simply hadn't found it yet. Whatever *it* was.

Closing up a box filled with antique dolls, he scanned the remaining pieces of furniture to decide which one to tackle next. One plastic-covered piece was taller than the rest, and seemed to sit away from the others. Maybe that was why it seemed to capture Dax's attention.

In any case, he stood slowly, his back slightly stiff from sitting on the floor, and then crossed the room. His skin bristled as he neared the tall piece. This was it; whether Adeline Vicknair was somehow leading him in this direction, or he simply sensed that he'd found what he was looking for, Dax had no doubt. Whatever was hidden under the heavy gray plastic was going to help him bring Celeste back.

Grabbing one side of the tarp, he pulled it to the floor

and viewed an antique oak chifforobe. A tall door formed the right side of the well-sculpted piece, and five drawers formed the left. He opened the top drawer and found it packed with papers and cards. He held the top one up to the light and saw a greeting card, so faded and yellowed from the test of time that the image on the front wasn't discernible, but when Dax opened it, the writing inside was intact.

Humbly and forever yours, John-Paul.

"John-Paul," Dax repeated. John-Paul Vicknair. He could see the name, not only on the card in front of him, but also on a paper he'd recently viewed. One of the Vicknair ancestry logs at the parish courthouse, he believed. Nanette had copied the handwritten parish records from the Civil War years in the hopes of finding someone living in the house at the time, and naturally she'd asked Dax to help her. John-Paul Vicknair had been one of the names from back then, from 1861 to 1865, which meant that the card Dax was holding was well over a hundred years old. He lifted several more cards and letters from the drawer, and found that all of them were either to or from John-Paul Vicknair, and that the other correspondent was his wife, Clara.

"*Mon dieu*, you scared me to death!" Nanette exclaimed, entering the attic.

He squinted at her in the dimness of the room. She squinted back, her eyes puffy and her black hair tousled from sleep. "I'm looking for something," he said.

"Looking for what?" The warped planks of the wooden

floor creaked loudly as she crossed the room to peer over his shoulder. "And this better be good. I thought a monster-size rat was roaming around up here, right above my bedroom. And do you know it's three in the morning? I have a herd of ninth-graders that would love to take advantage of a tired Ms. Vicknair tomorrow morning, and I don't like giving them the one-up on anything."

Opening the second drawer, Dax found more letters and cards. The third drawer yielded the same thing, as did the fourth and fifth. All were from John-Paul Vicknair to Clara, or vice versa, and all of them were apparently written during the mid-to-late 1800s, including those Civil War years that he and Nanette had been searching.

"I got a note from Grandma Adeline tonight," he said, still scanning the cards and letters as best he could in the limited light.

"A note? You mean another assignment?"

"No, a note, telling me that the information that you need is in the attic."

"The information *I* need?" she questioned.

"These cards and letters," Dax said, waving at the mound of them crammed in the drawers. "Some of them are from the Civil War. I know that may not prove anything, but you never know." He frowned. Maybe he'd been drawn to the chifforobe because it held what Nanette needed. Maybe what *he* was supposed to find was somewhere different entirely.

He turned and scanned the room again, while Nanette eagerly started thumbing through the letters.

"You think what we need for the National Register is in here? Proof that the house was inhabited during the Civil War? Seriously?" she asked, suddenly much more alert.

"I think that's what she was talking about, as far as you're concerned."

"What do you mean, as far as I'm concerned?" Nan asked, holding up a letter to the light.

"She said that the information I want is up here too."

"You mean about Celeste?" Nanette asked, surveying the letter in her hand.

Dax nodded, but she was too preoccupied with trying to read the letter to notice.

"I can't see anything up here," she complained.

"Yeah, I know." He spotted a couple of empty boxes and pointed to them. "Grab those, and we'll gather the letters and take them downstairs where the light is better."

He began scooping up the letters from the top drawer, waited for her to open the first box, then gingerly placed them inside. The paper was old, and in some cases already torn from age, or from their Vicknair ancestors rereading each other's correspondence. He moved to the other drawers and did the same, until both boxes were full. Then he rubbed his fingertips along the bottom of each drawer to verify he hadn't missed any letters. No way did he want to miss one that might help Celeste get back.

Looking at the boxes, both filled to the brim, he realized that while he may have found what they were looking for, identifying it was going to take time. And time was something he didn't have to spare.

"Want to take them to the kitchen?" Nan asked. "So we can spread them out on the table?"

"Sure. You're actually going to stay up with me?" he asked, knowing that she never voluntarily gave up sleep before a workday. She'd been telling the truth earlier; ninth-graders would make mincemeat of a tired teacher.

"I may read a few of them with you. Gotta admit, I'm curious to know what's in these letters." She grabbed one of the boxes as Dax lifted the other. "So you think there's something in here that will help you figure out how Celeste can stay longer?"

"I know that there's something in this attic that will help, and I'm thinking it may also be in these letters."

"Did you learn anything from Ryan?"

"Yeah," he said, motioning for her to start on ahead of him. "I learned that Celeste's situation is nothing at all like his was. He controlled when he came, where he went, how long he stayed, everything. She has no control, none at all. And there are other things that are different about her too, not just different from Ryan's situation, but different from every ghost I've seen."

He followed her out of the attic and used their time navigating the ladder and then the two flights of stairs leading to the kitchen to once more run over all of the differences he'd noticed—Celeste's exhaustion, her lack of control over when she came and went, the fact that she didn't glow as brightly as other spirits and her eyes weren't black.

Dax decided not to enlighten Nan that Celeste also

had the ability to touch him, and to do way more than that. She'd brought him to orgasm with her mouth, *in* her mouth. He hardened again, merely at the memory.

He placed his box on the table and immediately sat down behind it, so there was no way Nan could notice the bulge pressing against his jeans. She had no need to know those details, and Dax certainly had no desire to share them with his cousin.

He cleared his throat. "Ryan suspects that she glows brighter when she gets closer to the other side."

She placed her box across from his. "But every time our ghosts visit, they're already glowing, and the brightness doesn't increase as they get closer to crossing, or it hasn't with any of mine. What about yours?"

"No, never."

"And their eyes are always jet black, right from the moment I get them," she said.

"Mine too. That's what I don't understand about Celeste. Something's different, and unless I figure it out in time, I'm afraid she'll cross completely, and I won't be able to stop it."

"And you think these letters hold the answer for what's going on with her?" she asked, lifting a handful from her box.

"Hell, I hope so." He gave her a tired smile. "So, you up to reading, oh, a couple of hundred letters?"

She sighed, then put the letters back on top of the stack. "You know, I thought that I'd help you get started on them," she said, peeking at the clock on the microwave. "But I've got to get up in two hours. As much as I want to find proof that people were in this house back then, I do have a class to teach in the morning. And you have to work too, don't you?"

He did. In fact, tomorrow he had to cover his biggest route, visiting doctors in the majority of southeastern Louisiana. Typically, he loved his job. He made decent money, though currently most of it went toward repairs on the plantation, and he got a company-paid car—a BMW, no less—but it did involve a lot of driving and long hours, and generally required he get a full night's sleep before a day of work. "Yeah, I do. But I think I'll go ahead and start on some of these first, then I'll sleep. Unlike your teaching job, I don't really have a time I have to get started."

However, the later he started, the later he'd have to work, and in the back of his mind, he was hoping to see Celeste tomorrow night. Then again, his grandmother's note had said she'd need more than a day of rest before she could return again. Maybe he *should* work an extra-long day, in case she showed up later in the week, and he decided to take a day off.

Nanette yawned. "Tell you what. You look some of them over tonight and then mark the spot you get to. I'll pick up tomorrow afternoon. With the parent–teacher conferences out of the way, I should be home right after school's out, so that should give me plenty of time to see what we've got."

"Deal. And I can't help but think that what we need is in here," he said, indicating the boxes filled with letters.

"I hope so, because it'd be really good to put Charles Roussel in his place. I've been dreaming of the day when I can tell him that he has no control over whether the Vicknair plantation stays or goes." She smiled, apparently envisioning the scene with the cocky parish president. "Maybe you're right. Maybe Grandma Adeline has given us a way to save the house."

"Maybe she has." And maybe, just maybe, she'd given him a way to get back the woman he loved. One thing was for sure: if he got her back, he wasn't going to waste a minute. He prayed their next time together wouldn't be their last, but if it was, then he wanted to make sure he gave her every pleasure a woman could get from a man, and that each and every pleasure was as potent, as overwhelming, as what she'd so selflessly given him tonight—powerful enough for her to remember for eternity.

8

TWO HOURS LATER, Dax was on his second pot of coffee and still poring over the box of letters when Nanette entered the kitchen.

"You didn't sleep," she said, stating the obvious as she filled a mug with coffee, then walked over and topped off his cup.

"Nope." Dax peered into the remaining box of letters on the floor beside him; he'd been reading them as quickly as he could and still was only halfway done. It'd taken time to view them, because in most cases they'd been in their original envelopes, and both the envelope and the papers within were weathered and fragile. On top of that, the writing was fairly faint, though it could have just seemed that way because Dax's eyes were so tired.

Nanette sat across from him and surveyed the two piles of paper taking over the majority of the kitchen table. "Okay. Tell me what you found."

"These aren't dated and don't have any references to historical events that would date them, per se." He pointed to the larger stack on his right. Then he indicated the eight letters and envelopes on his left, the ones that she'd be most interested in. "But these—these are a different story entirely. It seems our great-great-great-great-grandfather—and I'm assuming I've got the number of greats right—not only fought in the Civil War, but also took the time to write his wife and tell her about it."

Nanette's green eyes practically gleamed. "And his wife was…"

"Right here," Dax said, glad that he was able to give her what she wanted, even if he hadn't found anything to help him with Celeste. "She stayed at home, at the plantation."

"No way! We can prove it? With those?" She reached for the small stack and pulled them toward her, protectively. "Dax, that's incredible!"

"Yeah, and I'm betting there are more in here that I haven't even gotten to yet, but these eight are all dated between April and May 1862, during the battles at Fort Jackson and Fort St. Philip, where the North was trying to get control of New Orleans and that portion of the Mississippi River. Pretty interesting stuff, really."

Dax had also found it interesting that John-Paul Vicknair had managed to write his wife daily throughout the ongoing battle, a sign, in Dax's mind, that all Vicknair men were singularly focused when it came to the women they loved. He'd bet John-Paul had been as determined to write that letter every day as Dax was determined to have Celeste with him, every day.

Nanette read the first letter, nodding as she scanned the page, then flipped it over. Then she read the second, and the third, and so on, while Dax worked on finishing yet another cup of coffee. It'd been a long night, and he did have to go to work soon. He knew that he'd never finish all those letters before he had to go. But he'd made a good dent, and he'd found what Nanette was looking for, so the effort hadn't been totally wasted, even if he'd yet to find anything that hinted as to why Celeste couldn't get back to him.

"So she stayed here while everyone else was fighting. He talks about his younger brothers, and his father, all joining in the Confederate efforts," Nan said. "And he thanks her for staying here, and for helping the spirits to cross."

"I know. That's exactly what we need, isn't it?" Dax asked. "Now you can attach those letters to the nomination form and send it on in."

Nanette nodded, but she was frowning, Dax noticed, and when she looked up, her green eyes were glistening, on the verge of tears.

"What is it?"

"We can't use these," she said solemnly. "I know you've worked hard to find them, and I'm really feeling terrible about going back to bed knowing that you stayed up all night going through them. But we can't use them." She leaned over the table to look in the box. "But there are more here, right? I'll keep going through them this afternoon. Maybe there's something in there that we can use."

Dax was dumbfounded. He had dates, battles, the

name of their ancestor who was fighting and the name of his wife at home. What more did she need? "Why can't we use them?"

"Because he talks about the ghosts in every one of them," she said. "If we send these as verification of—" she looked at the name on the letter "—Clara Vicknair living here during the Civil War, the committee will read the contents, and they'll learn that she was helping ghosts cross over. Whether they believe it or not, the next thing you know, everybody and their grandmother will be traipsing out here to see the haunted Vicknair place." She shook her head. "We can't do it, not with these. But maybe there's something in there that doesn't talk about the ghosts? Something that can be dated to the Civil War too?"

Dax could feel his frustration peaking. "Ever thought that maybe Grandma Adeline intended for us to use these? I mean, she's the one who said what you were looking for was in the attic. Maybe it's time to bring our ghosts out of the closet, so to speak. Would it be so bad if people knew? Especially if it helped us get on that register? That *is* the goal, right? And obviously, Grandma Adeline thought she was sending us in the right direction to achieve that goal."

"I can't believe that. She protected the family secret, like everyone before her. If what we need is really in these letters, then we haven't found it yet."

"Fine," Dax said, standing and taking his cup to the sink. "But I can't read any more letters now. I've got to get ready for work, and then I've got a full day visiting doctors."

Her chair squeaked as she twisted to look at him. "Did you find anything to help you with your problem? Anything about what's happening with Celeste?"

"Not yet." He stared out the kitchen window at the cane fields and wished Celeste was here to see the beauty of the sugarcane. Next week, the cutting would begin as they went through grinding season. Then the massive eight-foot stalks would be chopped to the ground, and the stubs burned to prepare the field for re-planting. It was an incredible, exhilarating process, and he wanted to share that with Celeste. He wanted to share lots of things with Celeste...if he could get her back. Unfortunately, not one line in any of the letters he'd read throughout the night gave him any indication how to make that happen.

"Well, we haven't finished all of the letters yet," Nanette said, evidently deciding on optimism as her method of handling their new dilemma. "I'll start on them after school, and I'll follow your lead here and make a pile of the ones that may help us for you to go through. Jenee will be here this afternoon too, so she can help."

"That sounds good," he said.

"You are going to sleep for a few hours before you try to drive all day, right?" she asked, shifting into her protective oldest-cousin role.

"Yeah, I'll catch a few hours before I start." He knew he was too tired to drive, and he could sleep four hours and still be on the road by ten. He'd let Nanette and Jenee tackle the rest of the letters this afternoon. Maybe they'd find something and have it waiting for him when he returned. If he was lucky. "Let me be lucky," he said softly as the cane reeds blurred together in the field. He squinted, thinking that he really was exhausted if his eyes couldn't even focus. But then, the air sounded different too, as if he could hear the reeds moving against each other in a soft, sweet cadence.

Dax leaned his head closer to the window to listen, then he unlatched it and pushed it open, trying to see if he could hear the song again. "Did you hear that?"

"Hear what?"

"The cane, moving. It sounds like—" he heard it again, crystal clear "—someone singing, maybe?" Then, as the sound intensified, Dax made out a few of the words. "Something about the leaves in the fall, fluttering to the ground."

Nanette moved from the table to stand beside him. "I don't hear anything. Are you sure it's the cane, or are you hearing a spirit?"

Dax closed his eyes and definitely heard a song, and a little girl singing it. "You're right. It's a little girl." He opened his eyes. "I've got another ghost coming." He typically heard ghosts for a day or so before their arrival, which meant that by tomorrow or the day after, he'd likely have another little girl spirit that would need his help crossing. And maybe, just maybe, she wouldn't come alone.

9

ON THURSDAY, three days after he'd found the letters in the attic and had first heard the little ghost singing, Dax steered his car along the darkened curves of River Road in an effort to get to the plantation, and to the assignment that he felt certain was waiting for him in the sitting room. Although he'd been anxious for the spirit to arrive, since he assumed her coming meant he might see Celeste again, he hadn't minded that it took her a few days to find her way to the Vicknair plantation. In the past three days, he'd crammed in a visit to each and every doctor's office on his route, even though that had meant sixteen-hour workdays, in order to justify taking some time off if Celeste reappeared.

And he truly believed if there was any way she could make it back through with his new assignment, she would, particularly if Grandma Adeline was willing to help.

He turned the Beemer into the driveway and the little girl's song grew so loud within his head that he had to concentrate to navigate the gravel road ahead. He'd left the house while it was still dark this morning, and it was dark again now, but he'd accomplished his task, clearing his schedule to allow several days to help the young spirit, and to, hopefully, spend time with Celeste.

The big, bold branches of the magnolia trees lining the driveway swayed slightly with the breeze from the levee, and the song in Dax's mind seemed to mimic their movement, chiming in about the colorful leaves of autumn. Her voice, a lyrical tinkling, echoed from the trees, and Dax wondered how the young spirit had died.

He'd expected to see her sooner. It didn't usually take this long between the time he heard the spirits and they arrived needing help. However, on occasions when a child was on his or her deathbed, he had heard the songs, or laughter, or tears of the final days. He assumed that to be the case now, and he prayed the young girl hadn't suffered as she died.

Where the driveway circled around a majestic oak, he noticed that in the past few days, the big tree had lost the majority of its leaves. Though still towering and formidable, it looked different with the missing foliage, no longer the picture of life, but of barrenness, of the way it felt to be alone.

The way Dax felt without Celeste.

"Let her come back with this ghost."

Moonlight spilled freely through the bare branches of the tree and cast snakelike shadows on the ground. The powers that be often sent signs before a spirit's visit, a hint of what was to come with a medium's assignment. He hoped the eerie vision produced by the massive oak wasn't a sign that this assignment wouldn't go the way he wanted.

He grabbed his briefcase and had barely made it out of the car when he heard Nanette's voice, calling from the porch.

"It just got here," she said.

"What?" The wind peppered him with leaves as he walked toward her.

"Your assignment. I was in the sitting room rereading some of the letters from the attic when it showed up on the tea service a few minutes ago. I tried calling your cell but didn't get an answer."

"I was probably already on River Road," he said. "Not much of a reception by the levee."

"Well, it worked out good then, didn't it? You were almost home." She took his bag when he reached the top of the porch. "Here, I'll put that up so you can go get your assignment. You hear your ghost?"

"Yeah, she's been singing all day," he sighed, pressing his fingertips against his temple; the song was even louder now than before.

"And? Have you heard Celeste too?"

"No, but I didn't hear her last time either. She just showed up with Prissy."

"Maybe she'll show up again," Nanette said hopefully. "And maybe she'll bring us more information on where to find the answers for saving the house."

"You still don't want to use the letters?" He entered the foyer, then started up the stairs toward the second floor with her following in his wake.

"No," she said, her dismay evident in the single word.

"What if Grandma Adeline expected you to? You have to believe that she meant for you to use them, particularly with the battles noted, the dates, the names. It's everything we need."

"Yep, everything we need, and then some." She laughed softly. "I'm considering it, but right now, I'm leaning toward adding those letters to every other secret we keep in this house."

Dax shook his head. "Your call, but I really think that she told us about them because she meant for us to use them."

"She also said that the attic held what you were looking for too, though, didn't she?" Nan reminded him. "And you haven't found anything that helps you with Celeste, have you?"

"Haven't had much of a chance to look, since I've been trying to do a week's worth of sales calls in three days."

"Well, I haven't found anything that would help you either," she admitted. "And I have kept an eye out as I read the letters."

"Thanks." He entered the sitting room, where, sure enough, a lavender-tinted envelope graced the center of the ornate tea service. "Guess it's time to see if I get one ghost, or two."

"I'll leave you to it." Nanette scooped up a box of letters from a side chair in the sitting room, then turned to go. "Let me know about your new ghost, and let me know if Celeste shows too."

"I will." Wincing at the little girl's song, now escalating to a near fever pitch, Dax sat on the red settee and reached for the letter, eager to get started on his assignment and to, hopefully, see Celeste again.

The door snapped shut with Nanette's departure, and Dax opened the envelope. The little girl's song immediately ceased, and he sensed that overwhelming peaceful presence, the sign that a ghost knew he was going to take care of her needs.

As usual, the letter smelled of magnolias and reminded him of Adeline Vicknair, the way her scent had always cloaked him when she hugged him, and how she used to sit on the front porch of the plantation when the big trees lining the driveway were covered in her favorite blooms.

He withdrew the three sheets of paper composing his assignment and quickly read the top one, his grandmother's letter on her trademark scalloped stationery.

Dax scanned the information and learned that the young girl's name was Angelle Millet and that the reason for death was cancer. That explained Dax hearing her for several days. More than likely, she had been on the brink of death, and her spirit was already trying to soar, even before the body had stopped breathing.

Requirement for Passage—Attending her funeral, checking on her parents, and viewing her elementary school's fall program being performed in her honor.

Dax nodded and smiled. No wonder she had been singing about the season; she was practicing the songs for the show.

He quickly scanned the sheet of rules and read the final sheet, the official document directing his grand-mother to assign Angelle to one of her grandchildren.

He picked up the pages and returned them to the envelope, placed it back on the tea service and watched it disappear. Then he turned, scanned the room and waited for Angelle to appear with a golden-haired beauty by her side.

"Hi," a crystal-clear voice said from behind him.

Dax shifted in the seat and saw a beautiful little girl, her dark skin accented by the traditional spirit glow, and her eyes alight with excitement. She looked to be around ten years old, with full cheeks, a wide smile and several long braids tipped in vibrant-colored bows.

"Look, I've got my weight back," she said, grinning. "And my hair!" She ran a hand down one of the braids and smiled. "Mama said I'd have long hair again, when I went to heaven. She was right, even if I haven't crossed the whole way yet. And Ms. Adeline said I'll get to see Mama again, and Daddy, and the kids at school. I'll even get to watch the play, right?"

"Yes, you will," Dax said, glad he could grant her request and trying his best to hide his own sadness at seeing her here, in this room, alone.

She nodded. "They promised me that, no matter what, they'd go to the fall program. We knew I wasn't going to make it until then—the doctors said so—but I wanted them to go. My friends are going to sing my song."

"Your song?" he asked.

"Yep." She bobbed her head. "I wrote it while I was in the hospital watching the leaves fall outside my window. It's a pretty song, I think."

Dax smiled. "Yes, it is."

"You've heard it?" she asked, her surprise evident. "How?"

"I've heard you singing it for the past few days," he said, "while I waited for you to come see me. And you're right, it's a very pretty song."

"So, what do I do? I can see Mama and Daddy getting ready to tell me goodbye." She shifted her weight to one foot and peered past Dax, and he knew she was checking on her folks.

"Think of them, and of how much you want to see them, and you'll go straight to them," he explained.

"And I can stay with them for the next few days, right? Until my school program on Saturday, so I can watch all of my friends sing my song, right?"

"Yes, you can," he said. "And if you need me, for anything at all, just think of me, and I'll know your thoughts. If you need me to come to you, then all you need to do is think of that, and I'll get there."

"You'll come hear me sing too, won't you? It's at Norco Elementary. Do you know where that is?"

"Yes, I do," Dax said. "It isn't that far from here."

"So you'll come? The program is Saturday night, two days away. You'll get to hear my song again if you come."

"Well, then, I wouldn't miss it."

Angelle smiled broadly. "Oh, I almost forgot. Ms.

Adeline said to tell you that—" She squished her nose as she apparently fought to remember something. "I knew I'd forget the name."

"Was it Celeste?" Dax asked. *Please.*

"Yes, that's it! Celeste. Ms. Adeline said to tell you that she was sorry, Celeste couldn't come back right now, but that she may be able to come for my program to hear me sing." She smiled brightly.

Dax sat down on the settee and swallowed thickly. She couldn't make it through. Why not? What kept her over there? And away from him? "Did she say why Celeste couldn't come now?"

The little girl shook her head, and her long braids swayed with the motion. "No, but I think she was just too tired. She looked very tired."

Leaning forward, Dax stared into her glimmering black eyes. "You saw her? You saw Celeste?"

Angelle nodded. "Yes, she was there, in the middle part, before I met Ms. Adeline. She's got beautiful long hair, doesn't she? And it's so blond that it nearly looks like gold. I really like the way it curls."

"Did she say anything to you?" he asked. "Celeste? Did she know you were coming here, and did she say anything to you? Or say anything at all that you could tell me?" Something that would help him know how to help her?

"I only remember her saying one thing, but I didn't know what it meant."

"What did she say?"

"She said, 'I need him,' and that was it. Just that she

needed somebody. But Ms. Adeline told her that she was still too weak, and she needed to get stronger."

"Did she say how long? How long until she'd be strong enough?" Dax asked.

"She said it'd be a few more days this time, and that made Celeste sad. I felt sorry for her because she really wanted to come with me. Maybe I could have helped her see whoever she needed to see, huh? Do you know who it is?"

Dax felt sick. "Yes, I think I do."

"Oh, look, there's my little sister with Mama and Daddy," she said, turning her attention back to what was happening at her home. "I'm going to them now. Thank you for helping me, and I'll see you at the show, right?"

"Yes, I'll see you at the show."

Dax watched her take a step toward the direction of her parents, then disappear. Then he let his head rest against the back of the settee in frustration while he looked at the ceiling and pondered why Celeste was so weak, and why no one, especially Adeline Vicknair, was able to help her through.

He swung out his arm and backhanded the tea service across the room. The pitcher clanged loudly as it pinged across the hardwood floor, as did the cups and the tray.

Placing his hands against his forehead, he scrubbed them down his face and embraced the aching throb over-powering his temples. It hurt like hell, and right now, it suited him fine.

He sat there in the stillness with his head cradled in

his hands and realized that life really did suck. Then he heard a soft *thunk* on the table, then another, and another, and he moved his hands away and opened his eyes.

The tea service was back in place, the tray in the center of the table, pitcher perched on one side and two dainty silver cups on the other, as though nothing had happened at all. But something *had* happened.

He'd had enough.

He glared at the tray and contemplated tossing it again, but it would just find its way to the table once more. Even his anger couldn't be sated in this damn room. "If you can't send her back now, then at least help me figure out what's happening to her, and how to help her stay."

Then, while he stared, a small lavender card, similar to the one Adeline Vicknair had sent three nights ago, materialized in the center of the gleaming tray with his name written boldly across the top. Dax leaned forward, picked it up, flipped it over and read the single line of text, written in his grandmother's definitive swirling script.

Patience, chère. *I'm doing the best I can.*

10

CELESTE PRACTICALLY jogged down the darkened path toward the middle. She hadn't felt this energetic, this lively, this *excited* in a very long time, mainly because she knew that Adeline Vicknair would let her pass back through. Celeste had no doubt she was strong enough now. She didn't know what had happened when she'd heeded the call of those voices, but whatever it was, it had strengthened her, and for that she was grateful. Plus, the crying had stopped, and she was grateful for that as well.

The only sound echoing from this passage now was her footsteps slapping against the cool stone as she ran. No sobbing. No screams. No pleading voices calling for her to come back. And the old saying was true—silence was golden—because their silence meant Celeste didn't need to go back to them, not right now. Right now, she could go where she wanted, and where she wanted to go was…to Dax.

She entered the middle room to find Adeline Vicknair, glowing brightly, her long silver hair floating around her head.

The older woman clucked her tongue against the

roof of her mouth disapprovingly as Celeste entered, but her dark eyes sparkled. She wasn't fooling Celeste; she was glad that she had returned, and she was almost as excited about letting her see Dax again as Celeste was excited to see him.

Celeste thought of him, the way he'd looked right before she'd been pulled away. His muscled body gloriously naked before her as he lay on the bed, the most tempting male she'd ever seen. Broad shoulders, even broader because of his arms tied to the post. His chest, heaving with thick, ragged breaths as she crawled on top of him and kissed that part of him that was so hard, so ready and so deliciously responsive.

She'd never thought she would have the nerve to do that to a man. No, that wasn't true. She'd dreamed of doing that to a man, if she ever found a man she wanted that much. But she'd had a fear, not of actually doing it, but of not doing it well.

She thought of Dax's powerful growl through his release.

Oh, yes, she'd done it well. And she'd do it again.

She was going back through to him today; one way or another, she'd make Adeline let her through. She had to. It'd been, what, two days? Three? She wasn't certain, having lost track of time when she'd rested down that other path, but she didn't care how long had passed. What mattered now was how long she could stay this time.

"You're stronger," Adeline said.

Celeste nodded. "Much stronger."

It'd nearly killed her when she'd found her way to the middle, saw the little girl—Angelle—on her way to see Dax, and wasn't allowed to go with her. She'd still felt weak, but she'd thought if she could just get to Dax, she'd feel better. But Adeline hadn't budged. Today, though, she would. Celeste would make sure of it.

"And your clothes," Adeline said, nodding. "I like the change."

Celeste looked down at the long, sage-green tunic. It was lightweight and sheer, with a feminine lettuce edging along the hem, and it was paired with a pair of winter-white capris that stopped at her calves. She was barefoot, like before, but her toes were painted a sparkling pink. Why had she changed from the white gown? How had she? She hadn't done it intentionally.

"Oh, *chère*, I'm sorry. I assumed you'd already noticed the new apparel. Evidently you were doing much better."

"Why do you say that?"

"Because they put you in regular clothes," the woman said matter-of-factly.

"Who put—" Celeste stopped when a pinprick of light forced its way through the middle wall, then grew wider and wider. "No. I'm not going."

"Oh, come over here, *chère*," Adeline instructed, wrapping an arm around Celeste, then pulling her to one side. "It isn't for you this time. Hurry. Several are coming."

The light grew brighter and brighter, bigger and bigger, until it claimed the majority of the wall and Celeste had to shield her eyes, and then a large mob of people appeared. Adults and children alike bustled through. They chatted and laughed as they passed, apparently oblivious to the two women standing against the wall.

The light grew even larger, even brighter, then absorbed them all, before going away. The scene reminded Celeste of the day when she'd been in the bus accident that brought her here the first time, with Chloe and all of the other children and counselors that were on their way to camp. Back then, Celeste had felt a pull toward the light, but she'd fought against its lure in order to stay and help Chloe, who hadn't wanted to go in until she saw her parents once more. Of all the times Celeste had seen the light, that time its draw had been the strongest.

She realized now that during every previous instance when she'd seen it, she'd felt some type of pull toward it, a desire to step closer and sink into it. But she didn't feel that this time, and she wondered why.

"Plane crash," Adeline said. "Red-eye flight. Most of them were sleeping and didn't feel a thing. One minute, they were asleep, and the next they were here, but it was their time, and they didn't have any unfinished business. If any of them had, I'd have needed to get some of the grandkids to help."

"Did Dax help Angelle?" Celeste asked.

"He's in the process of helping her." Adeline smiled. "Well, I say that he's helping her. The truth is, that little girl merely needed to be pointed in the right direction and told how to see her parents, and then she could take care of herself. Not a very tough case for my youngest grandson, but I typically send all of the children his way. He's so good with kids, like you."

"I wanted to be an elementary-school teacher," Celeste said.

"I know, *chère*. You'd be a good one, too." She tilted her head as though picturing Celeste in front of a blackboard. "I could see my Dax ending up with a teacher. The two of you would be a good match, but you already know that, don't you?"

"I want to see him," Celeste insisted. "I'm strong enough now, aren't I?"

"Yes, *chère*, you are, but last time the two of you tested your fate. You stayed too long, or exerted yourself too much—" she held up a hand "—and no, I don't know exactly how you became so exhausted so quickly, nor do I need to know. I'm just stating that if you want to stay longer on that side, with Dax, you'll need to practice some form of moderation in your activities."

Celeste grinned. "I promise—let me through now." She paused, then added, "Please." She waited, and when Adeline didn't move toward Dax's door, she said more firmly, "I'm not leaving this room until I see him, and I'm not going into the light. Not yet."

"I've never met another living soul so determined," Adeline said. "Well, I take that back. He's determined too, isn't he?"

"Yes, he is." Celeste stepped past Adeline and watched the doorway to the left, Dax's path, slowly open. "I can go now?"

"I won't stop you, *chère*. And don't get me wrong, I'm thrilled that you care so much about my Dax, and that he cares so much about you, but I don't want to see you hurt."

"Dax would never hurt me," Celeste said, hugging Adeline before starting down the darkened path.

"I'm not worried about him hurting you, dear," Adeline said, her voice growing faint as Celeste moved farther away. "I'm worried about you hurting yourself."

DAX ROLLED OVER, slammed a fist into his pillow and stared at the red numbers on the digital clock beside the bed: 3:27.

At least he'd slept for a few hours. That's more than he could say about last night, when he was so mad at the powers that be that he'd fumed and cussed all night long, not that it had helped.

Celeste hadn't come.

But exhaustion had prevailed tonight, and he'd slept a whopping four hours. Not bad for a guy this pissed, or this much in need of sex. In spite of the staggering orgasm she'd given him four days ago, Dax's body still burned for something more. He wanted to touch her, now that he knew he could. To run his mouth over every tantalizing indention, every curve, every nuance composing the woman who'd thoroughly captivated his heart, his soul. He wanted to taste her, the way she'd tasted him, and he wanted to feel her sweet heat surround him, to push himself deep inside and find out if they were even hotter joined together than they were when they touched.

"Damn." He growled the word with as much ferocity as he could manage and hoped that the powers that be were listening. There was no way Celeste wasn't strong enough to make it over again. She'd come back the very same day last time. Now she'd been gone four agonizingly long days, and he was tired of waiting.

"Is it that bad?"

He jerked around to face the owner of the voice who was standing near his bed. "*Mon dieu*, you made it through."

Celeste was glowing, shimmering, from the top of her blond head to the toes of her bare feet. Dax took her all in, the silvery-gray eyes that seemed to zero in on his chest before glancing down to where the sheet now pooled at his waist, the smile that set his pulse on fire, the curvy hips and legs that were showcased beautifully by fitted short pants…

She stood there and allowed him to examine her thoroughly, and to verify that he wasn't dreaming, then she smiled a little brighter. "I have new clothes." She waved a hand down her body. "No idea where they came from, but I like them."

"I like them too," he said, even though he couldn't care less about what she was wearing. She was here; that was what mattered. He wanted to take her and throw her on the bed, kiss her all over, then make love to her until she forgot that this was temporary.

Temporary. Did it have to be? And shouldn't he finally find out more about that before they moved on to hot and heated? The last two times he'd lost his senses and let lust rule, instead of asking the pertinent questions.

He'd regretted that ever since, not how much they'd wanted each other or how she'd satisfied him, but that he let her go without finding out how, and if, he could get her back on this side for good.

He swallowed and tried to ignore the fact that the sheet was now pitched in a tent from his hard-on. He needed answers, in case she was pulled away again. "Celeste."

"Yes?" she asked, licking her lips.

He cleared his throat. "I don't want to lose you again without finding out a few things. So, before we do—anything—I need to know. Where have you been? How did you get through? And how long can you stay?"

"I don't know where I've been," she said, stepping toward the bed. "I got through because of Adeline." She moved her hands to the hem of her long blouse, then crossed her arms in front of her as she brought it above her head, and let the green fabric fall to the floor. Like before, when she'd worn the silky white gown, she wasn't wearing a bra, and her nipples, like before, were tight little points, rosy pink and perfect for kissing, nuzzling, suckling...

"Celeste. Please, I need to know."

She put her hands to her waist, ran her fingertips inside the flat waistband of her pants, then slid them to the floor and stepped out of them. Last time, she'd worn nothing beneath her gown, but this time, a thin scrap of lacy white panties made Dax even harder.

"How long can you stay this time?" he repeated.

"She said it was up to me. If I can control my tired-ness, keep myself from becoming completely ex-hausted, I should be able to stay longer than before." She stepped closer to the bed. "I'm going to try to do that this time. I know it'll be hard, because I've honestly thought of nothing else but being with you, in every possible way. But if I feel myself getting tired—"

"Then we'll stop, and you'll rest," he completed. "We have to, Celeste. I need to try to figure out what's happening to you when you're gone, and I have a better chance of doing that if we work together and you tell me everything you remember about when you're gone."

"But I want you, Dax. I want you so much it hurts."

"Trust me, I know."

"So if I start feeling tired, I'll tell you, but right now, I'm not tired—at all. And since I'm not, we can talk about any questions you may have later, can't we? I want you, Dax." She eyed the tent in the bed. "And you want me too."

"Yeah, but—" He glanced at his hands, then smiled. "But what?"

Dax climbed from the bed and then motioned for her to get on top of the covers. "This time, I'm in control."

It was her turn to glance at his hands. "Can you, without touching?"

One corner of his mouth crooked up. For the past four days, he'd thought of nothing but how many ways he could, without touching. "Hell, yeah."

She crawled up on the bed, her heart-shaped bottom facing him as she moved toward the pillow, then turned around and licked her lips. "How can you?"

"You see, there's a loophole in that no-touching rule that I never realized until after you left last time."

"What loophole?" she asked.

Dax moved to the foot of the bed while she stared brazenly at his erection. He'd gone to sleep nude, and he was glad for it. Her skin was flushed and excited, tinged with a hint of pink, visible even in the midst of her shimmering glow.

He slowly moved up the side of the bed, careful not to touch her, not to let her know everything he was thinking, everything he'd be doing to her soon. Then he reached across her and braced both his hands on the headboard, his forearms within inches of her golden hair, tumbling wildly down her body. He'd feel that hair against him soon.

He grasped the headboard tightly, then brought his face to hers. "The part about me being able to touch, with everything but my hands." Then he lowered his body to press against her hot flesh and to his complete delight, the friction was just as sweet as before.

"Do you feel that, Celeste?"

She nodded, her eyes dilating with pleasure.

He moved his mouth to her forehead, kissed her lightly, and felt her skin scorch his lips. "Tell me," he said. "Tell me everything, what you feel, what you sense, what you want. I want to know." His words feathered across her temple as he nuzzled her hair out of the way and nibbled his way to her ear.

He licked the lobe, blew warm air on the dampened spot and demanded again, "Tell me, Celeste."

"I—" She turned her head so that her mouth rested against his. "I feel hot, burning all over."

He put his tongue against the corner of her mouth, then swept it slowly along her lower lip, while she gasped. Then he eased it inside and was rewarded with her hips bucking up to rub against his erection.

She broke the kiss and, panting wildly, said, "Please, Dax. I—I want this, all of this, but I don't know how much I can take. Please. I want to feel you inside of me."

Strengthening his grip on the headboard, he rose above her and peered into her eyes. They were still silver, still glittering with desire, and there was no sign of charcoal, or darker gray, or—heaven forbid—black. He wasn't about to rush his first time with her if he wasn't in danger of losing her.

"You can take a little more," he said, and her eyes widened. "Can't you?" he asked, and he moved his head down toward her breasts, but he didn't kiss them, not yet. First he moved his face beneath them, then bowed his head and rubbed the stiff peaks with his unshaven face.

Again, her hips bucked wildly, this time pushing against his abdomen, and he could feel her damp heat, hot and ready.

He moved his head, forcefully grazing her nipples

with his stubble, and he knew every sensitive nerve ending was being teased by each pass.

He looked up at her, saw her eyes were still silvery-gray, then took his tongue to the base of her breast and slowly licked his way to the tip. Her back arched off the bed as she pushed the tight point into his mouth, and he hungrily accepted her offer, sucking it between his lips, then pulling it between his teeth.

A sharp, piercing moan escaped her, and he felt her juices begin to flow between her legs.

"Need—you," she said on a gasp. "Please."

He looked back at her eyes, and though the change wasn't drastic, they were darker now, and as much as he wanted to make this last, he didn't want to push her too far. He couldn't lose her after one time, but he wasn't going to leave her this hot, this feverishly ready, either.

Pressing against the headboard, he lifted his body from hers, and she shook her head. "No, don't stop. Not now."

"I won't," he promised, shifting his weight so he could release his hands, bracing them on the bed on both sides of her, then lowering his mouth to her thigh. "Raise your hips, Celeste."

She did as he asked, pressing her heels against the bed and lifting her center.

Her scent teased him, and he nearly lost his fight to keep his hands away. He gripped the comforter in his fists, then lowered his head to her hip and ran his tongue beneath the tiny strap of her panties.

While she watched and moaned, he pulled her

panties off with his teeth, moving down one side, then the other, and kissing, nipping and sucking as he worked. By the time he had them at her ankles, her entire body was writhing, and her center was glistening wet and completely open…for him.

Dax took one more glance at her eyes, gray now, with no hint of silver anymore. But they weren't black yet, and he prayed they'd stay that way, at least until she came. He wanted to take this slow, but slow wasn't an option anymore.

"Now spread your legs, *chère*." She did, and Dax moved his face to her most feminine spot and licked.

Heat, fiery, blazing, sizzling heat met his tongue, made his lips burn, and he delved deeper.

Celeste arched her back, lifted her hips and pressed against his mouth, while Dax ran his tongue up her quivering folds to her sensitive nub, accessible and exposed and perfect. He kissed it, then he flicked his tongue over it while her hips rose higher and she moaned his name.

"Please, please, I'm…almost…"

He moved his tongue faster, then felt her body tense as she strained to find release and fell just short of her climax. He wasn't going to make her wait any longer; she was getting way too close to the edge, way too close to being taken from him again, and he didn't want to lose her yet.

He pressed his mouth against her hot clitoris and sucked it between his lips, then she screamed, vigorously riding his mouth with hard, quick convulsions, her sweet juices soaking her pulsing center. Dax slid his mouth toward her opening and licked the delicious treat.

While she shuddered through the last ripples, he continued to lick her, kiss her, adore her. Then, when her body finally stilled, he rose above her and saw her eyes, dark charcoal and glazed with fulfilled desire.

"That was wonderful," she whispered while he moved beside her, careful to keep his body against hers but his hands away from temptation.

"Yes," he agreed. "It was."

She closed her eyes, then slowly opened them again, and Dax could see the exhaustion claiming her spirit.

He frowned, and started to tell her, but she knew.

She gave him a soft smile, then reached out and touched his mouth with her finger. "I know. I need to rest now, or I'll be taken again." She nodded. "Don't worry. I'm not going to leave you too soon this time. I'll rest, but when I wake up…"

"When you wake up," he said, his mouth moving against her finger as he spoke, "we're going to talk."

She blinked, then gave him a sultry smile. "On one condition."

"Name it."

"After we talk, I want to know."

"Know what?" he asked.

"I want to know if there's any way possible that it could be even hotter when you're deep inside." She slid her finger from his mouth, then moved her hand to her womanhood. "I want to feel that heat…deep in here."

"Then promise me something, *chère*."

"Name it," she said, grinning as she echoed his words.

"You'll get plenty of rest now, because after you wake up, and we talk, you're going to need it."

_11_

THE SOUND OF Dax's stomach growling woke Celeste from a blissful sleep. She giggled as she rolled over, opened her eyes and viewed the beautifully naked man beside her on the bed. At one point during the night, he'd retrieved a silk necktie from the closet and asked her to tie his hands to one of the bedposts. They were still there, stretched above his head in a position that could in no way be considered comfortable. Safe, yes. Comfortable, no. But he'd said that he didn't trust himself to keep his hands off her unless they were otherwise engaged.

The thought that she had that much power over him sent an arrow of desire straight to her core.

"You know, I could get used to waking up and finding a guy all naked and tied up and waiting for me," she said, leaning above him and watching the way her glowing hair tickled his chest and his nipples promptly responded. "Even if his stomach does sound rather monster-like."

He smirked. "I'm sure you could, and I've done my damnedest not to wake you, even though it's well past lunchtime."

Lunchtime? She turned toward the windows and

realized that when he'd gotten up to get the necktie, he'd also untied the heavy drapes and let them completely cloak the room in darkness. "How long have we slept?"

"Oh, at least ten hours, but I'm going to have to leave this bed now, or I must admit rather embarrassingly, if I stay here much longer, I may wet the bed." He indicated his impressive erection. "I'm afraid it's not entirely due to arousal this time."

"Oh, I'm so sorry." She scrambled up the mattress to loosen the necktie at the post. Evidently, her knot-tying skills were improving if he wasn't able to slide his hands free. She grinned.

"Hey, it's not that funny," he chided, sliding his arms free, then wincing when his shoulders cracked and popped as he moved them gingerly back in place.

She covered her grin with her hand. "I'm so sorry," she repeated. "I could have slept over there—" she indicated the reading chair that occupied a far corner of the room "—and then you wouldn't have had to worry about accidentally touching me, or anything."

"As if I'd let you sleep anywhere but beside me while you're here." He gave her a reprimanding look. "Don't even think about it, *chère*." Then he climbed naked from the bed and grinned at her. "Besides, I'm not complaining. I wouldn't trade watching you sleep or feeling you against me for anything, but right now, duty does call."

He walked toward the bathroom while Celeste stared at his magnificent behind. Then he paused at the door and glanced back at her in a caught-ya-looking move.

"Hey, what can I say? I like what I see," she said.

"Me too," he said. "In fact, I like one thing very much, your eyes are silver again."

She scooted across the bed and rose on her knees to see her reflection in the mirror above the dresser. Sure enough, her eyes were silver, not black like the other ghosts she'd seen. Funny, she'd never thought to look at them before, but apparently Dax had, and he'd noticed the distinction between her and the other spirits. "What does that mean, that they're silver?"

"It means you've rested well," he said. "They turn darker when you start to get tired, and then, when they turn black…"

"I go back?"

"Yeah."

"Have you ever seen another ghost with silver eyes?"

"Nope, and neither has any of the other Vicknairs. Nan and I have started a list of differences, in fact, while we've been analyzing some letters from the attic."

"Letters?" she asked, still staring at her image in that mirror and still not quite adjusting to the difference. She didn't look like herself with these odd-colored eyes.

"I got a note from Grandma Adeline telling me that what Nanette and I needed was in the attic. We've been looking for proof that the house was inhabited during the Civil War. That'll give us a better chance of saving our home."

"Saving it? From what?"

"It's a long story, but basically, ever since Katrina hit,

the parish president has the power to remove all hazardous structures, and for some reason, he doesn't want to give us the time we need to get this place fixed back up. Nan and I are trying to get it put on the National Historic Register to tie his hands. But while we were looking for that, I've also been trying to find answers about why you're stuck in the middle the way you are. Grandma Adeline said that what Nan *and* I were looking for was in the attic. Granted, I've been helping her try to get information about the house, but I really thought she was referring to your situation, and I also really thought that those letters would help."

"And they haven't?"

"No. Well, not yet, anyway. Then again, there's no reason for me to worry about getting information from those old papers while I've got you here. Surely we can figure this out together, and we'll start with the list Nanette and I have made of differences between you and other ghosts."

"Okay," she said, holding her hair back and then tilting her head one way, and then the other, to get a better look at the odd-colored eyes. "What *could* it mean, that they're different?" When she was living, her eyes had been green, the same bright green as both of her parents', and her older sister's, Nelsa. She frowned, and realized that she'd never see their green eyes again. Then she wondered…*why wouldn't she?* Prissy had been allowed to see her parents again, and now Angelle was doing the same thing. Why hadn't she been given another chance?

She climbed off the bed and moved toward the mirror, bringing her face close to the reflection so she could properly survey the strange hue. The gray eyes weren't unappealing or anything like that; they were unique, like the silver marbles she and Nelsa had played with as children. But they weren't *her* eyes, and that realization made her stomach queasy. "What does it mean?" she repeated.

He'd already entered the bathroom, but he'd evidently heard her question. "Well, that's easy. It means you're special," he called.

"Special," she repeated. Funny, she didn't feel special; she felt confused.

Dax exited and winked at her as he crossed the room, and his stomach, once again, roared. He grinned, picked up a pair of jeans from the top of the dresser and slipped them on. "I'd love to start up again," he said, zipping them as he spoke, "but now that you're rested, I'm going to have to eat first. Do you know it's past three in the afternoon? And besides, I do want us to try to talk a bit as well, and put our heads together to figure out exactly *why* you're so special."

"There's something different about me, isn't there?" she asked.

"Everything about you is different, Celeste. Unique and exceptional and distinctive…and addictive. And quite honestly, I'm hooked already. Hell, I don't want to let you leave again. Ever." He grabbed a white T-shirt from the top drawer of the dresser and pulled it over his head, then waited for her. "Wanna come down to the kitchen with me? Then maybe we can go for a walk outside and talk—try to figure some of this out."

"And find a way for me to stay, you mean?"

"That's the plan."

"And then, after we talk," she said, picking her shirt up from the floor, "we can make love." She slipped the gauzy fabric over her head and then grinned.

He stepped toward her, then waited while she shimmied into her panties and pants. Then he gave her that crooked, sexy smile that she loved. "That's definitely in the plan."

"So, do you think I know something, or have seen something, that can help you figure out why my eyes are silver, and why I'm stuck in the middle?"

He opened the door and let her pass through first. "I don't know if you can help me or not, but I know we need to try. He paused at the doorway, then stuffed his hands in his pockets and moved closer. "Hey, my hands are safe."

"So they are." She laughed, then lifted on her toes and arched against him, bringing her mouth to his and accepting another of those hot, passionate kisses that made her forget her limited time here, forget her exhaustion, forget everything but Dax.

She let her body lean completely against his, and he chuckled softly. "You realize you're doing amazing things for my ego, if merely a kiss leaves you that weak-kneed."

"Well, believe me, Dax Vicknair, it does." She didn't elaborate that she really felt the need to sit down, or to go back to sleep. And they'd slept longer than she'd ever slept in her life.

Why *was* she so tired?

"Come on, let's go to the kitchen."

He led the way down the hall, then down the stairs to the kitchen. Celeste followed, trying to focus on something besides the fact that her legs didn't want to cooperate. She noted the warped wooden steps along the way. Some bowed slightly; others dipped inward. They creaked and groaned against Dax's weight, and Celeste wondered if the stairs were all that safe.

He paused at the foyer, turned and saw her examining the rickety staircase. "Don't worry. We haven't had anyone fall through them yet."

"I *was* wondering."

"I know. They're a hazard, but if you take a look around, the whole house is. When we go outside, I'll show you the front porch, and the fact that all of the columns are slightly leaning in various directions, and that one side of the house actually seems to have been pushed in a bit from Katrina. All of the rooms on this floor are closed off," he said, indicating the plastic sheeting that covered the entrances to three rooms off the foyer, "except for the kitchen. And that's because we like to eat too much to shut it down for any length of time." He shrugged. "I guess Charles Roussel, the parish president, does have a case for wanting to knock this old house to the ground, but we're getting there. The new roof is done, and we'll just take the rest of it one step at a time. Shoot, this place has been around too long, and meant too much to our family and the spirits, to let it go without a fight. Plus, I met you here."

His words touched her soul, and she leaned toward him and brushed her lips to his. "I'd love to stay here, with you, forever."

"Can't think of a thing I'd like better either," he said, those hazel eyes staring into hers, which reminded Celeste that the eyes he was seeing weren't even remotely like hers.

She swallowed, and decided to think about something else for now. Turning away from him, she indicated the plastic-covered doorways branching off the foyer. "What are you doing to all of the rooms down here?" she asked.

"We just finished cleaning them up enough to pass the inspection from the local historical society. They were worried about post-hurricane contamination since the bottom floor of the house flooded during Katrina, but we passed the test. Eventually, we'll open the rooms back up and restore them completely. They need new floors and some paint. And furniture would probably be a nice touch," he said with a laugh. "We can probably take care of that with a few trips to the attic, I learned this week. But for now, we've kept the demolition crew at bay, and that's what counts. Thankfully, they're completely slated with work in Jefferson Parish for now and haven't planned to check our status again until next year, which is good, since we're tapped out on funds for the time being." He sighed, then started down a hallway that led to the back of the house and the kitchen.

She followed him though the swinging door leading to the kitchen and watched him rummage through the cabinets. Like the remainder of the house, the mahogany cabinets had seen better days; they were scuffed and scratched, with many of the doors missing hardware, as in the handle to the cabinet Dax was opening.

"Are these the letters you found?" she asked, indicating a small stack in the center of the kitchen table.

"Those are just a few of them, but they're the ones that indicated specific times and dates when one of our ancestors was living in the house during the Civil War."

"Which is what you need, right?"

He smirked. "That's the way I see it, but Nanette's still deciding whether she wants to share them. See, every letter there refers to the spirits, and she can't decide whether she wants folks to know our little secret." He placed a long loaf of French bread on the counter and cut it in half with a serrated knife, then moved toward the refrigerator and withdrew several plastic bags of deli meat. "Anyway, enough about Nan and her dilemma. It's the list there, on the yellow notepad, that I want you to look at." He tossed the meat next to the bread, then removed bottles of mayonnaise, mustard and relish from the side door of the fridge.

She grabbed the edge of the pad and slid it toward her, but couldn't take her attention off Dax, and his ease in the kitchen. She'd heard Cajun men could really cook, in the kitchen and in the bedroom. She already knew about Dax's talents in the latter, and undoubtedly, he could fend for himself in the kitchen too. He was merely fixing a sandwich now, but she could envision him by the stove, a big pot of something spicy simmering in front of him.

He surveyed all of the items on the counter, nodded as though deciding he had everything he needed, then started making a sandwich that, in Celeste's opinion, would feed a small family. "Read that list and tell me if you can think of anything else. Hey, read it out loud. That'll help me see if Nan and I missed anything."

She cleared her throat, then began, "'Silver eyes. They darken as she gets tired, and turn completely black, like other spirits' eyes, before she is pulled back to the middle.'" Celeste looked at him and asked, "What color are they now?"

He turned away from the counter, tilted his head and said, "Pale silver, almost transparent. You must have rested well."

She nodded. She *had* slept well with him by her side, but she had also felt tired before they came down to the kitchen. However, right now, sitting here and scanning the list, she didn't feel the least bit fatigued, and that was good. She really wanted to stretch her time out with Dax. "I did sleep well." Then she continued down the list. "'No control over when she comes or leaves,'" she read, and added, "True." Then she read the next item, a single word and a question mark. "'Clothing?'"

"Yeah. I wasn't sure about that, but Ryan said he had the ability to change his clothing at will. Basically, he thought about what he wanted to wear, and his attire changed. But when I first saw you in the summer, you were wearing a yellow tank top and jeans the whole time. I assumed that's what you were wearing when you…" He paused, and she knew why. He didn't want to admit that she'd died.

"That was what I wore the day of the wreck," she said, helping him out of the uncomfortable sentence. "And you're also right about my clothing. I don't know how it changes, or why. That white gown that I had on the last time I visited you wasn't anything I had when I was living. And these—" she waved her hand down her side to indicate the sage tunic and capris "—I didn't own anything like this either. Not that I don't like it, or anything like that, but this isn't typically the kind of thing I'd have picked out to wear. In fact, it really looks like something more along the lines of what Nelsa would wear."

"Nelsa?" he asked, and momentarily took his attention off the sandwich he was creating.

"My older sister," she said, smiling as she thought of Nelsa. At twenty-five, she was four years older than Celeste and truthfully closer than just a sister; she was Celeste's best friend. "Nelsa has always had a real flair for picking fashionable clothes," she said. "Me, though, I was more of a tank-top-and-jeans kind of girl. The outfit you saw me in during the summer was basically what you'd always see me in, but this is pure Nelsa." She looked at the gauzy, feminine shirt again. "I always

wanted to dress more like her, tried to, actually, but
never could really get a handle on her style. I guess it's
that younger sister thing, always looking up to her and
all. She was the levelheaded one, the girlie-girl and the
one with the cool taste in clothing. I was more of a
tomboy, a little—or maybe a lot—more reckless, and I
had a tendency to bend, or outright break, the rules." She
smiled. "Do you think I'm in clothes like Nelsa's
because I always admired her style when I was living?"

He paused, seemed to consider it, then asked,
"What about the gown? Was that something she'd have
picked out?"

Celeste laughed. "No, that's the type of thing my
mother would have picked out. She always got that
sweet, virginal-bride kind of sleepwear when it came to
buying gifts for me and Nelsa. I guess in her eyes, she
was trying to keep us young and innocent." She shook
her head. "Okay. Maybe I wore that as a tribute to Mom,
and this as a tribute to Nelsa?"

"But you said you can't change your clothes at
will, right?"

She closed her eyes, thought of her favorite green
tank top and worn jeans, then opened them. She still had
on the tunic. "No, I can't."

His brows drew together as he seemed to try to
process this new bit of knowledge. "Write that down by
clothing," he said. "That your clothing seems to be a reflection of the people you were closest to. Maybe that
means something, even if you don't have the ability to

change it." Then he turned his attention back to the sandwich, spreading mayonnaise across one side of the bread and mustard along the other, while Celeste added the new information, and thought about her family, particularly Nelsa.

"I miss her," she whispered. "Nelsa always kept me in line, or tried to. If I'd have listened to her this summer—" Her lip quivered, throat tightened.

"What?" he asked.

"I wouldn't have been on that bus, and I'd probably still be breathing. The counseling position was actually for teachers who were already working in the school system, you know, not for brand-new college graduates who were merely eager to get started. I saw the opportunity to travel to those camps and work with kids, and I went ahead and put that I was employed as a kindergarten teacher." She shrugged. "I lied because I didn't want to wait until the fall to start working with children. I mean, I did my internship in the spring, during my last semester, and I loved it. Why would I want to stay away from kids for the whole summer?"

"Didn't the people running the camp check your employment claim?" he asked, and she nodded.

"Yeah," she said with a guilty grin. "But I *was* employed by the school they checked. I'd already accepted a teaching position there, beginning this fall, so they answered that I was employed by the school. Luckily, the fact that I hadn't done anything but my intern duty there never came up." She sighed. "If I hadn't lied on that application, and if I hadn't been on that bus, I'd be teaching now." A tear pushed forward, and trickled down her cheek, and she brushed it away.

Dax dropped the knife, and it clanged on the plate as he crossed the room and kneeled beside her. "I'm going to get you back, somehow, and you will get to teach. Ryan came back to this side, and if he can do it, then you can too. We've just got to figure out why your situation is so different than his was, and what we have to do to make it happen. But I swear, I won't give up until we do." Then his brows furrowed, and he stared at her cheek. "Celeste?"

"What?" she whispered, then wiped another tear away.

"Ghosts don't cry."

She blinked, and another swell of tears spilled free. "Well, I do." Then she sniffed, and managed a smile. "Want me to add that to the list?"

"Yes. Definitely."

She wrote it at the end, then she peered past him to the sandwich he'd barely started making. "Go on and finish that. You need to eat."

He exhaled thickly, then nodded and returned to the counter. "We will figure it out," he said, more to himself than to her, but Celeste nodded, and returned her attention to the list.

"The next thing is another question," she said. "And I don't understand it."

"What does it say?"

"'Can she see me?'" Celeste read, then looked toward him. "What does that mean?"

"When you're in the middle, can you see me, on this side? Because ghosts can typically see those they care about when they're on the other side. I've never met a spirit that didn't say something about watching the ones they love."

She shook her head. "Well, you've met one now. I can't see you, and I can't see my family either. I can't see anyone when I'm in the middle."

"What about here? When you're on this side with me, can you think about your family and see them? Because that's the way it works, you'd see them, and go to them, if you wanted to visit them again."

She'd thought of that earlier, and had tried to picture them. "No, I can't. I can't see them at all." She fought another impulse to cry, and wrote that down as well, finishing the list. "That's the last thing you had," she said, watching him spread a layer of olive paste on top of the mustard, then stack pastrami, salami and provolone cheese on top of it. He topped that off with the other half of the French bread, then brought it to the table.

"Can you think of anything else to add?" he asked, leaving the plate to go grab a napkin.

"No, I can't," she said, eyeing the massive sandwich. There was something about it…

He sat down and noticed where her attention had fallen. "I feel awkward eating in front of you when you can't, but if I don't eat, I'm not going to be good for anything later."

Celeste grinned, knowing what she meant by "good

for anything." He might as well have said "good for everything," because *that's* what she knew he'd give her when they were together intimately again. Everything.

"I'm not hungry," she said. "I promise." She was telling the truth; she wasn't hungry, really, but she did miss the ability to eat.

"I can't do this," he said. "You *are* hungry. I can see it on your face."

"No." She shook her head. "I promise I'm not, but I think I've tried that kind of sandwich before, and if I remember right, I liked it very much."

"It's a muffuletta. Surely you've had one."

She recognized the name at once, though she'd heard it only that one time, that one day. "I had one in New Orleans, before the group boarded the bus heading to the camp." She paused, then smiled at the memory. They'd had a lot of fun that morning, Celeste and the other counselors with the young campers. A lot of fun, until the bus crashed.

She saw realization dawn on his gorgeous features, the brown depths of his eyes showing intense compassion.

"You're talking about the day of the crash," he said softly. "That day?"

She nodded. "That was the first time I tried a muffuletta, and I really liked it." Then she forced a smile and decided she wanted to change the subject, not necessarily because it bothered her, but because it bothered him. "Did you know the brown in your eyes shows more when you're worried? But when you're excited, they're practically all green." She grinned, even though he was obviously still thinking about the day of that wreck. She lowered her voice. "And when you come, the gold takes over, those tiny flecks practically glow when you completely let go."

Mission accomplished. *That* took his mind off the first time she'd eaten a muffuletta, the last time she'd breathed. In fact, his hazel eyes shifted from dominantly chocolate brown to deep emerald green, and those gold flecks were present on both irises. Celeste loved his eyes, loved everything about him, in fact—his dark brown waves that seemed to always tease his forehead, and his mouth—have mercy, he had such a sensual mouth.

"What are you thinking?" he asked, taking a bite of the sandwich. "As if I didn't know."

"I'll show you…later. For now, why don't we talk about this list and see if we can't figure something out while you eat your sandwich."

He took another bite, and Celeste stood and moved to the refrigerator, then withdrew a Coke. She brought the can to the table, popped the top, then placed it in front of him.

"Thanks."

"My father never remembered to get something to drink when he ate, either." She returned to her seat and smiled, remembering her father. "You'd have liked him, and he'd have really liked you. He always tried to act like the big, burly tough guy in a house dominated by females, but once you got to know him, you'd have seen that he was more of a teddy bear than a grizzly." She laughed softly. "Yeah, you'd have liked him."

"He's passed on?" Dax asked.

"No," she said, shaking her head and wondering why she'd referred to her father in the past tense. *He* wasn't the one who was dead. "I guess I'm just assuming that you'll never meet him, you know, since that'd be kind of difficult to explain."

His brows dropped a notch, and he took another man-size bite of sandwich. Finally, he swallowed and frowned. "I would like to meet him. I think he'd like to know that his daughter is still hanging out here, and maybe he'd even have an idea why."

She chewed her lip, shook her head. "That'd just upset him, and I really don't want to hurt him anymore. He, Mama and Nelsa were so happy the last time I saw them. They saw me off when I left for the camp. My parents didn't even realize that I wasn't technically supposed to go. Nelsa knew, but even though she wasn't keen on me bending the rules, she knew how much I wanted to be with those kids, so she kept my secret." Suddenly, she remembered...

"You know, there's something else that I should probably add to this list."

"What's that?"

She wrote it down first, then read aloud, "Had the ability to cross, at first, but chose not to."

He chewed his bite of sandwich and swallowed thickly, then asked, "What do you mean? This summer?"

She nodded. "I saw the light and felt it pulling me toward it. It was as big and bright as I've ever seen, and the other people around me, people from the same crash, were going on through. I even heard them laughing and chatting after they entered. They had no fear whatsoever and really seemed happy to get to the other side."

"But you didn't go."

She shook her head. "There was that beautiful little girl standing over to the side and scared. She was trembling all over. The other kids weren't scared at all, they were actually fine with heading on into the light, and I heard grandparents, and other family members, I suppose, calling them on in. But she was fighting it, and didn't want to go. And I didn't want to leave her. She kept saying that her folks were going to take her to the beach, and she really wanted to see it before she left them, and she wanted to see them again, too."

"Chloe," Dax said, obviously remembering the little girl's request before she crossed over, to visit with her parents again, and to see the beach before she crossed. Her request had been granted, and Dax had consequently spent a week with her and her parents at the beach so they could communicate with Chloe before she crossed. Celeste had stayed with them that week too, to keep Chloe company, and she'd also fallen in love with Dax.

"Before I decided to stay with Chloe, I know I could have gone into the light, but I chose not to. I chose to stay with her. And then I met you, and I've been fighting the light's pull ever since." She smiled. "Now I don't go through because I don't want to leave you."

Dax leaned forward, apparently putting these new pieces into the puzzle he was trying so desperately to figure out. "But when Chloe went back to the light, you left, too. That's when I thought you must have crossed over. Where did you go?"

"I saw the light, and I watched her cross, but again, I wasn't ready to go. I knew if I crossed, I'd lose all chance of seeing you again."

"But you went somewhere, right? Where?"

"I don't know. There's another path that branches off from the middle. It's dark, and a little scary to go down, but that's where I have to go to rest. That's all I know. And during those two months when I was away from you, I didn't rest enough, or I'd be stronger now. I only went down that path a few times, and I never stayed very long. I guess I was afraid I wouldn't be able to find you again if I did. I don't know, since I can't remember what happens when I'm there. But during most of those two months, I stayed in the middle and tried to get back to you. Do you think—" She wasn't sure how to finish the question.

"What?" he asked.

"Do you think if I wouldn't have been going to that camp, wouldn't have been in that wreck, that I'd have never met you? I mean, in real life? What if the only way for us to be together was for me to die?"

Dax shook his head as he spoke. "No, I can't believe that. I think—I believe—that if two people are meant to be together, if they are truly soul mates, then they'll find each other, someway, somehow. And I can't believe that this is the way we were meant to find each other."

"Gotta admit, it'd be a unique story to tell people about the day we met," she said, then laughed, and was glad to see his gorgeous smile at that comment.

"Yeah, I think we'd beat all other first-date stories, hands down, though I'm not so certain many people outside of my family would believe it."

"I think you're right, though. I'd have found you, met you, somehow. Our paths would have crossed. I was so excited about where my life was headed, I'd gotten the job I wanted, and then I was going to follow through with the rest of my plan."

"The rest of your plan?"

She nodded. "Fall in love and settle down. That was all that was missing, and if I'd have met you, I could have taken care of that as well."

He'd only eaten half of his sandwich, but he stood, took the plate to the counter and wrapped the remainder in aluminum foil, then put it in the fridge. "Come on. Let's go for a walk and chat. I want to hear more about your family, and anything else that might give me a clue about how to help you stay longer."

"I thought you were starving. Don't you normally eat all of your sandwich?"

"I normally eat two that size," he said, smiling. "But I've had enough right now. I don't want to waste any of our day together. In all honesty, we really don't know how long we've got. I mean, we can try to stretch this out as long as possible, make certain not to exhaust you and cause you to have to leave before you absolutely have to go, but until I can figure out how to keep you here, I'd rather spend my time getting to know you better." He held out a hand toward her, then frowned and stuffed it in the pocket of his jeans. "Damn rule."

"It's okay," Celeste said, standing and placing her fingertips against his cheek. "I can touch you, and as we learned last night, you're pretty good at touching me without your hands, aren't you?"

He leaned toward her, nuzzled her neck with his mouth, then slid those hot lips against her ear. "Hell, yeah."

She laughed and held out her arm. "Look what you did." A waterfall of gooseflesh trickled down her arm.

"Okay, that definitely belongs on the list. I know I've never seen a spirit with goose bumps."

"Maybe you just haven't touched them the right way."

"I haven't touched any of my ghosts in *any* way," he said.

His comment reminded Celeste that he still had a ghost that he was helping, unless Angelle had already crossed. "Before I forget, has Angelle's school play happened yet? I told her I'd attend if I could, and since I'm here, if it hasn't happened, I'd love to go. I'd always thought that it'd be fun to help my students put on something like that, and she was such a cute little girl, and so excited about her classmates singing her song."

Dax glanced at the kitchen clock. "Actually, her play is tonight, and thankfully, it doesn't start until eight."

She turned to see the time. "It's four-thirty now."

"Exactly, which gives us time to visit a little longer, and to do—other things—before the show."

"Other things?"

"Oh, yeah," he said, his suggestive tone holding a promise that she couldn't wait for him to deliver. "Come on," he continued. "I want to show you the levee, and the outside of the house, and I want to find out as much about you as I can before you have to leave again. There's got to be something I can do to keep you here, or at least get you back."

Her throat tightened at the reality of her limited time here. Maybe Dax was right; maybe by learning more about her, he could figure out what went wrong when she died, and whether there was any way she could get another chance at living, or at least another chance at staying with him.

He led her through a small mudroom that branched off the kitchen. Several wall hooks held rain gear, as well as a few gardening tools, and two deep, oversize sinks occupied one wall. A faded snapshot of a woman pruning a large shrub had been matted and framed and hung on the wall directly above the sink. Celeste recognized the striking woman immediately, even though she was much younger in the photo than when Celeste saw her yesterday. "Adeline."

He paused, looked at the picture and smiled. "Yeah, she always loved tending to her flowers, particularly her poinsettias." He pointed to the shrub. "I haven't seen any around quite as large as the ones we have here. I'll show you."

Celeste leaned toward the photo again to examine the shrub. A poinsettia? Since the picture was black and white, she couldn't tell whether the flowers were red, but they didn't appear to be darker than the others. "Are you sure?"

He stopped at the door. "About what?"

"That that's a poinsettia. I've never seen one that big, and I don't see any flowers on it."

"That's because poinsettias don't have flowers," he answered with a grin. "The modified leaves at the end that most people *think* are flowers are actually called bracts." He shrugged modestly. "They were my grandmother's favorite flower, and she wanted the grandchildren to keep them a part of this plantation almost as much as she wanted us to keep the ghosts around. She liked the smell of magnolias, but you couldn't keep her away from her poinsettias when she was gardening. Come on and see, then you'll understand."

Celeste followed him outside, and immediately noticed what he was talking about. Huge shrubs spanned the entire side of the plantation and were covered in red-tinged blooms—or bracts.

"They're just starting to turn now, but in a couple of weeks, this will be a sea of red, and cover the entire perimeter of the house."

"They're incredible," Celeste said, taking in the beauty of the shrubs, towering nearly to the second floor of the home. "How tall are they?"

"They're only supposed to get to a maximum of ten feet or so, but I think ours are hitting twelve now." He tilted his head and looked down at her. "You've never seen poinsettias growing outside?"

"I didn't even know they'd grow outside of a pot," she said honestly. "And I don't think they'd grow at my parents' house."

He grinned. "Sure they would. They love the climate here."

"But I don't think they would there." Her reply was drowned out by an older-model red Camaro that pulled up the driveway and then parked. A striking woman with shiny jet-black hair climbed out. She wore a black sleeveless mock turtleneck and black pants, and she looked like...a Vicknair. It wasn't so much that her features reminded Celeste of Dax, but there was something about her eyes, and the way she studied Dax before she even spoke, that told Celeste this lady knew that this house, and Dax, had secrets.

"Who's with you?" she asked, moving toward Dax and Celeste.

Dax grinned. "What makes you think someone's with me?" He didn't even look at Celeste when he spoke, so she remained silent. She wasn't sure whether he wanted this lady to know she was here, Vicknair or not.

"For starters, you haven't been out of your room all day, and that's not like you, even on a Saturday, so I assumed you had company. Then there's the fact that I haven't seen you with a genuine smile in months, but you've got one now. And of course, there's the other…"

"The other?"

"You've had sex and—" she tilted her head and lifted one brow "—I think you've currently got sex on the mind now. Yep, I'd say that's a given."

Dax shuddered. "How you do that is beyond me. And it's not right."

The woman smiled triumphantly, and she was even prettier when she smiled. "So, you must be Celeste," she said, basically speaking toward the poinsettia shrub and not missing the mark by much; Celeste was only a foot to the left of where she was talking. "I'm Nanette Vicknair, the oldest cousin around, and evidently, one of the few who hasn't found the means, or the desire, to become intimate with our guests."

"Nice to meet you," Celeste said, giggling. While Nanette was trying her best to sound as though she was issuing Dax a reprimand, the absolute glee in those sparkling green eyes betrayed her.

"She says it's nice to meet you," Dax relayed. "And by the way, she's onto you. You can't fool anyone into thinking you're not glad that she's here, and that she's with me."

Nanette shrugged guiltily. "You're right. I'm glad you came back, Celeste. He's been an absolute pill to be around since you left. And hey, I am getting more accustomed to ghosts in the family every day."

Celeste's chest clenched. Ghosts in the family. She

wasn't in the family and didn't know whether it would even be possible. But wouldn't that be nice…

She looked at Dax, and he looked at her.

Nanette cleared her throat—loudly. "So, what are you two doing out here?"

"I was showing her the poinsettias," Dax said. "And then we're going to take a walk on the levee."

"Out of curiosity, have the two of you had a chance to discuss our list, or maybe check out the letters for more clues about what's happening with you, Celeste? I'm sure Dax has told you that your situation is far from the usual of what we deal with around here."

"We just finished discussing the list, and adding a few things to it," Dax replied.

"And?" Nanette asked.

"And we know that something's different, but we still can't figure out what that is."

"Well, I'll keep thinking about it too," she promised. "Don't worry, Celeste. If Monique found a way to get Ryan here, Dax will do the same for you. He's amazing at figuring things out, and believe me, he won't stop until he's got all the answers." She paused. "And speaking of figuring out answers, I'm going to go through all of those letters again, see if we missed any that might have mentioned the Civil War without mentioning our unique guests." She took a step toward the house. "You two enjoy the levee."

"We will," Dax said, and the slight quirk of his mouth told Celeste that he planned to enjoy more than its views.

"You know, it's getting darker earlier now," Nan continued. "So you shouldn't waste time. You'll want to see the barges on the Mississippi and the wildflowers that are still blooming near the cane." She looked at the bounty of red-tinted leaves behind Celeste. "But then again, there's nothing across the road that's prettier than the poinsettias. In all of Grandma Adeline's wedding pictures, these big shrubs provided a vivid red backdrop. She said she had a Christmas wedding just so she could show off the flowers."

"Technically, they're not flowers…"

"Oh, hush," Nan said, interrupting Dax before he could get started. "I know they aren't flowers, but they look like flowers to me, and they're even prettier."

"Yes, ma'am," he said, saluting her as she started walking away.

"All right, smart-ass, that's enough." She climbed the steps to the mudroom. "And by the way, I am glad you're here, Celeste. It's nice to see Dax smile again. And if you do get the chance to come back, we'd love to have you."

The door slammed as Nanette entered the house, and Celeste shivered.

"Are you cold?" he asked.

She smiled. "No. I don't think I can get cold now."

"Then what is it?"

"I guess I'm a little scared," she said honestly. The fear wasn't so much about what was going to happen, but from not knowing, and apparently having no control over, whatever would happen. "Do you know what's funny?"

"What?" he asked, moving closer to her with his hands firmly stuffed in his jean pockets.

"I told Nelsa that when I got married one day, I would want a Christmas wedding. The bridesmaids would wear red, and they'd carry poinsettias. I didn't even know they could grow this big, or I'd have wanted to get married in a place where they could surround me, like this one." She squinted as she viewed the bushes and tried to imagine those red-tinged leaves turning even more boldly crimson and covering the old house like a floral blanket. It would be incredible to see, and a breathtaking location for a Christmas wedding, the kind of wedding Celeste had always wanted.

And now she didn't merely see a Christmas wedding, with poinsettias and red dresses, but she also saw the image of her groom, waiting to give her everything she ever desired...*Dax*.

12

DAX TOOK in the beauty of Celeste's shimmering hair
billowing behind her as she looked out over the mighty
Mississippi, its dark water churning steadily and splash-
ing softly against the levee's edge. It was an incredible
image, the woman he loved standing in the midst of the
place he loved.

Even with its shaky foundation, the Vicknair plantation stood prominently on one side of them, and the
waters of the Mississippi bordered the other side. In the
distance, large, flat barges noisily trudged their way
down the river, and a late-afternoon breeze filled the air.
The sky was gradually shifting to the typical shades of
a Louisiana late afternoon and early evening, dark blue,
deep purple and rose.

And in the center of it all was Celeste.

"This is amazing," she whispered. The cane reed
swayed behind her and the wind gently whistled through
it. "It's breathtaking."

"Exactly what I was thinking."

She smiled, stretched out her arms and let the breeze
ripple against her loose blouse. The fabric pressed

against the gentle curves of her breasts and emphasized her peaked nipples.

Dax's groin tightened.

Then she looked down at the ground beneath her feet and wiggled her toes.

He glanced back at the house, at the long gravel driveway, then at River Road, separating the Vicknair property from the levee. "I didn't think about you not wearing shoes." He squatted beside her to look at her dainty feet.

"They don't hurt," she said, still gazing at the scene around her. "It's so beautiful here. I want to remember this forever, Dax."

He didn't look up. Instead he continued looking at her feet, thankful he could hide how the piercing reality of her statement had devastated him. She wanted to remember this forever because she assumed that she wouldn't be able to see the beauty of his world on a regular basis. He simply wouldn't believe that there wasn't some way that he could make it happen. He just had to put the pieces together.

"Oh, Dax, look at the sun now," she said breathily.

Still kneeling beside her, he turned his head to see the sun had dipped a little lower, its color converting from golden yellow to rich orange, an amazing contrast to the blues, purples and pinks of the surrounding sky. She was right; it was beautiful. But he couldn't stop thinking about her time for this visit, undoubtedly running out, and the fact that he still didn't know how to bring her back.

She lowered to her knees beside him and smiled. "Evidently whoever decided on my new clothing didn't think I needed shoes. Hey, stop feeling bad. I'm not hurt."

"I should have offered to carry you."

"Kind of hard to do that without using your hands, don't you think?"

"Hell." Again, the reality of their situation was driven home to Dax. "Someday, I'll carry you."

"That a promise?" Her eyes—currently a bit darker than they'd been in the kitchen—glittered, and her long curls tumbled wildly around her shoulders. He wanted to run his fingers through her hair. One day, he would.

"Yeah, it's a promise." He didn't know how, but one way or another, he was going to hold her, carry her, love her…permanently.

"But what about today? What do you plan to do for me today, Dax Vicknair? Because, since you did forget to carry me across the road and all, even though I was fine on my own, I think you owe me *something*." Her finger touched his chin, tilted it slightly, then her mouth moved closer. She slanted her lips over his, then hummed her contentment when he opened his mouth and their tongues met.

Dax hungrily accepted her kiss, hot and potent and tantalizing, while he gripped the earth with his hands. If he didn't, he'd grab her and hold her and never let her go. And who knew what the powers that be would do if he blatantly ignored the rule? They could take her away forever, and Dax wasn't about to take that chance.

She broke the kiss, licked her lips, then glanced at the folded blanket he'd grabbed from his car and dropped on the ground nearby. Knowing they would be making love at some point during this walk, he'd wanted to make it as comfortable as possible for her, but after learning that she hadn't felt any pain on her bare feet, maybe she wouldn't need the cushion after all.

"If you don't need that—" he started.

She pressed a finger to his mouth. "I don't, but it was sweet of you to bring it, and I want to use it." Her touch, as always, sizzled against his dampened lips, and he sucked the tip into his mouth.

"Amazing, isn't it?" she asked.

He kissed her finger. "What?"

"How hot it is, with us. It's not normal, is it? The heat that I feel when I touch you, and when you touch me?"

He grinned. "Well, it certainly isn't anything I've ever experienced before."

"Me, neither," she said, then added, "I wonder, if I were breathing, would it be this hot?"

"What do you think?" he asked, and moved his face closer to hers, so close that he whispered his next words against her lips. "Do you think there's any way it wouldn't be hot between us?"

She gave him a siren smile. "No way at all. But I can think of something that we haven't done yet that might make it even hotter."

He swallowed and wondered…

Celeste evidently guessed his thoughts. "I'll be

careful," she said. "If I feel myself getting pulled away, I'll tell you."

"I'm not ready to let you leave me, and if it takes that much out of you that if things do get hotter, then we may not have any control over that pull."

"You're not saying no, though," she said, not really asking a question. "I want you inside of me, Dax, no matter what. And if I feel like I'm slipping away, we'll slow things down."

He grinned. "So in the heat of the moment, if you say slow down, I'll just—stop. Just like that."

"You can, can't you?" she asked.

"I can *try*," he said. "But trust me, it won't be easy."

"Well, maybe you won't have to stop at all. I have rested and I am definitely ready to expend a little energy."

"A little?"

"Okay, a lot." She stood and unfolded the blanket, held it up to catch the wind, then let it fall to the ground behind some shrubs that still had a few leaves. Then she kneeled on top of it and motioned for him to join her.

Dax slid his body against hers and brought his lips to her throat, nuzzling her hair out of the way as he brushed soft kisses along her neck and beneath her ear. She rubbed against him, her body growing hotter with every movement, and Dax leaned away from her, then looked at her eyes.

Smoky gray. The light shimmering around her was a little brighter too, more of a pale yellow than the creamy glow that had surrounded her for the majority of this visit.

She was getting weaker.

He licked his lips, swallowed, and wondered whether there was any way possible to do this, to do everything, without forfeiting all of her time.

"Don't," she said. "Don't even think of stopping now, Dax. I need you. Please, I'll tell you if we need to stop."

"You'll tell me," he repeated.

She nodded, then grabbed the edge of his T-shirt and slid it up and over his head, her hands scalding his flesh with the movement. The heat of her, the heat of the two of them together, had Dax's mind and body soaring. He needed to be inside of her, needed to be one with her, but he also needed to keep her here. "Celeste."

She didn't respond, but instead moved down his body, quickly removing his shoes and socks and then turning her attention to his jeans. Her hands were frantic and shaky as she unfastened them. "Don't say it," she said. "Let me have you, Dax. Let me be with you and know what it's like, please."

Hell, he didn't want to deny her anything she wanted or needed, and obviously, right now, she needed him. But what if that need took her away?

"You want me too," she said, removing his jeans. Then she placed her hand against his heart, and the heat, once again, penetrated his entire body as she slid her palm down his abdomen and stroked his erection. "Don't you?"

"Yes, but…"

She shook her head, those long spirals gently swaying with the action, then she removed the gauzy blouse. "No buts, Dax. I can do this, and I'll tell you when I start getting too weak. But I want to be with you, and I'll never forgive myself if I leave again without knowing how it feels to have you inside." Then she stood and shimmied out of her pants and panties.

With her hair flowing behind her, she stood above him, boldly and beautifully nude. "I want you, Dax." Her words were true, Dax had no doubt of that, but they also held a hint of apprehension.

She was nervous, whether about making love, or about the possibility of her being pulled away during their lovemaking, he didn't know. But both of those things were on his mind as well. He knew they'd fit beautifully together, and that their lovemaking would be off the charts; hell, her kisses alone made his entire body burn. But if he lost her…

She lowered to the blanket beside him and then pressed a soft kiss fully against his mouth, then she pushed into him, so that he slowly lowered his back to the ground and let her have control, obviously what she wanted.

Dax fisted his hands in the blanket and used his mouth, his thighs, his body to move against her as she climbed on top of him. Her eyes, dark gray, peered into his, and he bit back the impulse to tell her to slow down. She needed this, and she didn't want him to make her stop. He'd simply have to watch her and try to protect her if she started getting too close to the other side, if those eyes started turning black.

Straddling him, she leaned over, that beautiful blond curtain of hair forming a glowing golden waterfall that tumbled past her breasts and teased his chest. Her soft, wet heat against his flesh caused his erection to harden to the point of pain.

He clenched his jaw and fought for control. She needed to take this at her pace, and if he rushed her, and then caused her to leave again, *he'd* never forgive *himself*. Slower was better, this time. "Celeste?"

"Yes?" She ran her fingernails down his sides, then back up again to cross his nipples, while Dax hissed in a breath.

"I'm not usually this—eager—but I want you so much, Celeste, and I'm not going to last long at all." He winced, and decided to go for the whole truth, since she'd figure it out soon enough. "Hell, I'm probably going to come the minute you touch me. But that might not be a bad thing this time, since it might help you to stay."

She leaned forward, braced her palms on his chest and giggled. "I wonder how many guys have used that excuse for explaining why they don't last very long," she teased, then cleared her throat, lowered her voice to imitate a male and joked, "Honey, I could last all day, but I'm going to do this quickly, so you won't be pulled to the other side."

Her blatant humor surprised him, and delighted him.

Without meaning to, he'd taken some of her nervousness away, and her eyes—thank goodness—had lightened a little with her laughter.

"For the record," he said. "I *can* last, but this first time…"

She leaned down and, still smiling, claimed his mouth. This kiss started playfully, with her nipping his mouth and grinning, giggling lightly as she explored his lips, but Dax felt her growing hotter as she deepened the kiss, using her tongue to explore his mouth and accepting his thorough exploration of hers as well.

Her body moved against him in perfect harmony with her tongue. She moaned, and that seductive sound teased every other part of his body as well. His hands clenched with the desire to touch her, and his erection ached to push deep inside of her.

But he wasn't in control now. In order to have some minor ability to stop this if it got out of hand, he had to give Celeste the lead. How far they went, and how fast or slow, was all up to her.

As if sensing his mounting tension, she broke the kiss and leaned above him, her breasts flushed and excited, and her hair glowing, illuminating the remainder of her body even more. "What do you want, Dax?"

"I want everything." That was nothing shy of the truth.

Her mouth curved into a smile. "Okay. What do you want first?"

He eyed her rose-tipped nipples. "I'll start with those."

She leaned over him, offering him a pebbled nipple.

Dax wasted no time drawing it within his lips, running his tongue around the tip, then sucking it between his teeth. Her back arched immediately in response, and he felt her grow even hotter and even wetter against his erection.

Her hips began to move, undulating in anticipation of what they would be doing soon, and Dax knew she was creating that sweet friction between his flesh and her core that would drive her closer to climax. He turned his attention to her other breast, licking it, nibbling it, and then sucking it between his teeth. This time there was no denying that she was almost there. Her intimate flesh was drenched now.

"Dax," she gasped, "I need—" she moved up and down his body, teasing his hard length "—you." Then she eased the tip into her heat and clenched her teeth while she held him there, at the brink of ecstasy.

He forced himself to look at her eyes, but they were closed. How dark were they now? "Celeste," he said, but she was too into the sensation to hear him. "Celeste," he repeated.

She looked at him, and those eyes were dark charcoal. "I—" She eased down a bit, and her face tensed.

Dax froze. He didn't want to hurt her. He glanced down his abdomen and saw that he was barely inside of her at all. "Celeste, we can stop." He had no idea if she'd tensed because of pain, or because of fear, but either way, no matter how much it killed him to do it, he *could* stop, for her.

She gave him a slight smile. "It's been a long time," she said. "I'm sorry I'm so tight."

"No, don't be sorry." He could feel the sweat beading on his forehead and upper lip. How long could he sit here and look at her above him, with merely the tip of his cock inside of her moist heat. She was getting hotter now, and he could feel her easing open, getting ready for him.

"Celeste, maybe we shouldn't do this now. I don't want to hurt you, and I don't want to be the reason for you crossing over, either."

"I need you. I need to know how it feels to have you be a part of me, Dax, even if I only get to experience it once. I don't want to stop, but—" She eased down a little farther, and to Dax's horror, tears trickled from her eyes.

She wanted him, in spite of the pain. But he had no doubt that she shouldn't try to force this. Her eyes were darkening now, probably due to her determination to make this work, and to make love, at least once, before she crossed.

He couldn't deny her what she wanted, and he believed he knew how to help her through the pain. "Celeste?"

"I can do this," she said, then she pushed down on him, and winced. "I want to do this. I want you, Dax. I do. I'm just not used to it. And, honestly, you're really big."

He couldn't fight the smile at that remark. "I wasn't going to tell you I didn't want to do this," he said. "I want to, as much as you do, but you're not ready."

"Yes, I am," she argued, and before she decided to

press her tightness farther down, and force him to lose all control, he shook his head.

"That's not what I mean. I know you're ready emotionally, but you aren't ready physically, and I think I can help."

She pressed both palms against his chest, then slowly moved back up his cock. "How?"

Dax shifted his hips to remove his length from her. "Let me help you come, Celeste. That's what you need to take me inside." He licked his lips. "Let me taste you, *chère*, and help you come."

She sat up and tilted her head as though trying to figure out exactly how to situate themselves on the blanket to let him do what he wanted.

"Turn around," he said.

Her dark eyes grew big, but she did as he asked. And then, to his complete shock and delight, she announced, "If we're doing it like this, then I want to taste you, too." She shifted forward, bringing her mouth to the tip of his penis and placing her sweet center exactly where he wanted it, close enough to taste. She was already wet, and Dax had no doubt he could make her drenched and more than able to let him in, deep inside. He just prayed that she could stay on this side, stay with him, after he took her where she wanted to go.

She licked the base of his cock, then kissed the length of him, swirling her tongue around the tip before taking him in, and while she did, Dax kissed her intimate center, then licked, nibbled and kissed his way to the sensitive nub that he knew would give her what she needed. He concentrated on each sound she made, the moans that told him where she was the most receptive of his touch, and the sharp gasps that said she was ready to soar. Those, as he'd learned last night, were produced each and every time he flicked his tongue over her clitoris, so he did it again and again, then reveled in the tightening of her entire body, and then the pulsing convulsions and sweet juices produced by her orgasm.

She'd long since forgotten tasting him, her senses apparently completely absorbed in what he was doing to her, which was just as well. This time, he wanted to come…right here. He licked the very spot, and then was welcomed with another gasping climax.

Another kiss to her center, and then he asked, "Do you think you're ready to take me now, Celeste?"

He didn't have to ask twice. This time, when she moved down on him, to Dax's delight, she eased him all the way in, her center slick and hot and right. Then she looked at him, and her eyes had moved beyond charcoal into a carbon color that was way too close to the black he was dreading. "Celeste, we need to—"

She braced her hands on his chest and lost herself in the rhythm, moving up and down his length with exquisite friction, her gasps and moans escalating with every push, every pull, every clenching of her intimate walls. "No," she said. "I can't stop. I want to feel it—when it happens—and when you fill me up completely. Let me—have it all. I want you inside of me, coming inside of me. Let me feel it. Let me have—you."

Her words pushed away his reserve, and the spiraling tension built higher and higher, hotter and hotter, until Celeste tossed her hair back, thrust her breasts out and yelled his name.

The sight of her, the woman he'd wanted more than any other, losing complete control—with him—and giving him everything she had, everything he'd wanted for so long, sent Dax over the edge. "I love you, Celeste," he said, desperate to tell her now, desperate to make sure she knew. "I—love you." His orgasm rocketed through him, and through her, and then the illumination of her spirit blinded him, and her black eyes bore into his soul. She screamed his name once more… and was gone.

13

CELESTE COLLAPSED on the cold stone floor and closed her eyes. She was drained, emotionally and physically. He'd made love to her and it'd been the best thing she'd ever experienced, so wonderful, so magical, that she hadn't been willing to let him stop, even though she could feel her spirit being pulled away. She'd wanted to be with him so much, just once, that she'd given everything she had. And now she had nothing left. No way to fight the pull of that light.

Or could she?

She lifted her head from the floor and glanced at the doorway to Dax's world, closed solid, and she knew better than to expect Adeline to open it for her anytime soon. Besides, even if it were wide open now, Celeste didn't think she had even enough energy to crawl through, much less walk. And what about the light?

She looked toward that middle wall and half expected the big, golden door to open and swallow her up, but amazingly, it remained closed…for now. She shut her eyes again and hoped it stayed that way, long enough for her to rest and to get back out of here, back to Dax.

How long would she have to rest this time before she could make it back through? Or would she ever be able to go back again?

Tears trickled down her cheeks, but she didn't bother wiping them away. She was too tired for even that. She was so cold. Her body shivered, and the coolness of the floor against her tear-dampened cheek seemed to intensify as she lay there, wallowing in her misery. She'd had Dax, and she'd lost him.

"I love you, too," she whispered, but she knew he couldn't hear her.

Would he ever?

Celeste heard laughter, then sensed a hint of warmth in the room. She opened her eyes to see Angelle, giggling as she watched the pinprick of light on the middle wall grow.

"Look!" she exclaimed. "It's nearly time!"

Like before, the light grew bigger and bigger, until Celeste's cold spirit was bathed in blissful warmth. It felt so good that she couldn't stay away, and she inched closer to it.

"I thought I'd see you at my program, but Dax said you were gone. He looked really sad," the little girl said. "Hey, are you hurt? Do you need help going in?"

Celeste blinked. Did she need help? Yes, she did, though not the kind of help the sweet girl was offering. She wasn't ready to go into that light, not yet, no matter how good it felt. And Angelle had seen Dax at her program. Celeste was supposed to have gone to the play with Dax, or she had planned to, but she hadn't been able to resist the temptation of truly being with Dax in order to stay longer.

More tears fell, and she let them.

"I'll help you." Angelle walked toward Celeste, then moved behind her and wrapped her arms tightly around Celeste's chest. "I'll get you there," the little girl said, slowly pulling Celeste backward toward the ever-growing light.

Celeste tried to drag her feet and slow Angelle's surprising progress, but she was so weak, and the little girl was suddenly very strong. "No, Angelle," she whispered. "Don't—want—to go."

Angelle loosened her hold, but they were already so near to the light that Celeste could feel the pull of its warmth, and another draw, one that was so forceful that she was having a very difficult time fighting its allure.

But she would. For Dax.

"I can't go in yet," she whispered, then she turned to see Angelle's face, and gasped.

Several children's faces had formed within the light, and they all smiled and reached for Angelle.

"You should come with me," Angelle said. "They say it's amazing there. We're going to go play. Isn't that awesome?"

"How—how do you know them?" Celeste's voice was so weak that she could barely hear herself speak, but Angelle heard.

"From the hospital. We all knew we were coming here one day, and we promised to help each other when it was time to go. Now they're here to take me inside. Don't you want to come?"

Celeste shook her head. "No, sweetie. Not yet."

Angelle eased Celeste back to the floor. "You sure you're going to be okay here? I really do think you're supposed to come with me, you know."

"I'll be okay." Celeste assumed that was the truth. She really didn't know whether she'd be okay or not. Would she languish here in this room forever because she was fighting that light?

"Okay." Angelle squatted next to Celeste and hugged her. "Thank you for everything. And you know what?"

"What?"

"I'd have liked you for a teacher. You'd have been a really good one."

Celeste's eyes watered, and she nodded, not knowing what to say.

Angelle stood, and Celeste watched several of the children in the light reach out and touch her arms, then pull her inside. "Bye!" she yelled, then her glowing body joined the light, and all of their faces disappeared.

But the light didn't go away, and Celeste soon saw why. Another hand reached out and moved toward her face, and she was too weak to even back away. If it pulled her in, she'd have to go. She simply had no more strength to resist.

"Not yet," she whispered. "Please, not yet."

The glowing hand came closer and slowly pushed her hair away from her face, then one finger tenderly brushed a tear away, then another. The palm moved to her forehead, then gently smoothed down the length of Celeste's hair.

She *knew* that touch, could almost picture the man who'd always caressed her hair that way.

"Granddaddy?"

The hand moved to Celeste's cheek, and brushed more tears away. Celeste had no doubt that her grandfather, the kindhearted man who had died when she was fourteen, was now taking care of her once more. Stroking her hair. Drying her tears.

"Not yet, Granddaddy. Please. I want to be with him. I can't leave, not yet."

Pausing for a moment, the hand touched Celeste's cheek once more, then disappeared. The light disappeared with it, leaving the middle room—and Celeste—in complete darkness.

She heard the voices down the path to the right. They were screaming something, but she was too spent to determine what the words were.

Was it her name?

Maybe, maybe not. She couldn't concentrate enough to be sure.

Was it possible to actually end it all in the middle? To stay right here, freezing cold and unable to move, unable to speak, and then simply stop existing? Because *that's* what she felt like right now, like if she stopped thinking, stopped listening, that she would merely fade away. No more voices. No more light.

And no more Dax.

She couldn't let that happen, Celeste realized as her eyes grew so heavy that she couldn't keep them open. She fought that, too. How would she have a chance at going back down Dax's path if she couldn't even keep her eyes open to see the way?

The shivering intensified and reminded her of that type of uncontrollable shaking that occurred when individuals were in shock, or intense pain. She'd seen a lot of people go through that on the day of the bus wreck. Was that what was causing her to tremble from head to toe, her teeth audibly chattering and the chilling sound echoing off the walls of this room? Or was she simply cold? Or tired?

Or fading from existence?

Don't! she mentally screamed, trying to force her eyes to remain open. But in spite of all her efforts, her spirit lost all ability to fight the inevitable, and her lids slid closed.

_14_

DAX WIPED his forearm across his sweaty brow and stared at the piles of brown and gold magnolia leaves lining the driveway. He could · have waited until Saturday, when all of the cousins would come to the plantation for their weekly workday, to rake the mountains of leaves. No doubt the job wouldn't have been so difficult with a few more hands, but then his muscles wouldn't be aching, his back wouldn't be hurting and his body wouldn't be covered in hard-earned sweat.

Right now, he wanted to ache, hurt and sweat. He wanted his body to feel, the same type of misery that his soul was feeling.

For the past three weeks, since the day Celeste had disappeared, he'd worked sixteen-hour days six days a week, in an effort to keep himself so busy he wouldn't remember how badly he hurt.

It hadn't helped. He'd only had more time behind the wheel to think about the precious few hours he'd spent with Celeste, and to think about how barren his life would be without her.

What if they'd permanently exhausted her spirit from that last visit? Had she crossed over completely because she didn't have the strength to fight it anymore?

He dropped the rake, took off his gloves and flung them away, then saw Nanette's car heading up the driveway. She slowed as she neared, rolled down her window and cleared her throat.

"It's Wednesday," she said.

"Right." He really wasn't in the mood for small talk, or even a sarcastic *"Tell me something I don't know."*

"Okay. So, it's the middle of the week, and you don't look as though you've been to work today." She glanced behind her. "And judging from those piles of leaves, you've been raking all afternoon."

When Dax didn't comment, or ask her point, she continued, "Well, I'm glad you finally decided to take a day off. You've been working yourself to death ever since—well, for the past few weeks."

"Working myself to death?" he questioned, scoffing at her odd choice of words, particularly when their family dealt with the dead on a regular basis. "Not quite. And I didn't willingly take a day off. My regional rep ordered me to take the rest of this week and all of next week off to relax. Seems he was tired of explaining why I was showing up twice as often as normal."

She smirked. "Well, good for your regional rep. But if you're supposed to be relaxing, you've got a funny way of going about it. Why didn't you wait until we could help you with all of that?"

"Didn't want to." He could have said more, but of the things he didn't want to do right now, talking about Celeste topped the list.

"Fine. Well, I'm going in to start dinner. I had a heck of a day at school, by the way, in case you're interested. It started with one of the sophomores accidentally stepping on the gas instead of the brake when he was trying to park his car, and sending the thing into the building near my classroom."

Dax's eyes widened. "He okay?"

She laughed. "He's fine. Shook up, but okay. So don't worry, he shouldn't be visiting you anytime soon."

"That's good." Dax was glad the boy was all right, but he did hope that he got another ghostly visit soon. He figured it would better his chances of seeing Celeste.

"Leave the piles, and we'll bag them later," she said, then drove off.

Dax decided to take her up on that offer. He'd been raking the majority of the afternoon, and he was ready to head inside and cool down. True, it was November now, but in Louisiana, while some months might be cooler, they all fell pretty much under the same classification—hot.

He picked up his discarded gloves and slapped them against his jeans to remove the excess dirt, then he grabbed the rake and started heading toward the work shed behind the house. Rounding the corner of the porch, he stopped walking to take in the scene. Red. Everywhere. His grandmother's prized poinsettias blazed crimson and towered against the side of the house in a brilliant hedge that would be worthy of a *Southern Living* cover photo.

Grandma Adeline would be proud. And Celeste would be awed.

"I told Nelsa that when I got married one day, I wanted a Christmas wedding. The bridesmaids would wear red, and they'd carry poinsettias. I didn't even know they could grow this big, or I'd have wanted to get married in a place where they could surround me, like this one."

With Celeste's words echoing in his thoughts, Dax turned away from the poinsettias and continued to the shed. He deposited the gloves and rake, then used the rear entrance of the house. He didn't want to walk past those poinsettias again.

Nanette stood near the stove and spooned rice into two deep bowls, then covered it with gumbo out of a huge black iron pot. Her smile beamed as she turned. "You cooked, and it smells fabulous."

Dax nodded. He'd done plenty today to keep himself busy. Cooking the gumbo had only been one small part of it. He'd also started sanding the floor in the front room that used to be a formal parlor. Right now, it was merely another empty room in need of repair. Good thing the place had plenty of them; he'd find an ample supply of work to keep his mind off Celeste. Then again, that hadn't worked today, had it?

Nanette moved the bowls to the table, then got some drinks from the fridge. "Come on, I'm starving."

"I need a quick shower first, then I'll head back down."

"Well, hurry, before the gumbo gets cold."

He nodded, left the kitchen and started toward his room, but he didn't really care if the gumbo was cold. He had no appetite, for gumbo or anything else…except Celeste. His hunger for her was palpable, and quite possibly would never be satisfied.

With that still on his mind, he entered the shower. As each hot droplet of water covered his skin, he remembered Celeste's trembling hands, her warm mouth, her sweet kisses. It'd been three weeks, and he hadn't gone one minute of that time without thinking of her. Right now, in fact, he could see her so clearly, the way she'd looked when they'd made love. Those golden curls tumbling wildly around her as her body moved over his, her mouth caressing his neck, nuzzling him as her sweet, hot center accepted every inch of him.

He could almost hear her softly moaning, then those moans turning into sharp gasps as she thrust her hips and brought him deep, deep within her. And he could feel the tensing of her flesh around him, holding him so tight as her climax grew imminent.

Dax bowed his head and closed his eyes as the hot water pelted him. Then he circled his cock with his hand in an effort to reproduce what was happening in his mind. There, she was riding him, fiercely determined to claim every inch of him and to bring him to the same kind of powerful orgasm that was building within her.

In reality, Dax was finally succumbing to his baser

needs. Three weeks was way too long to go without a release, and one minute was way too long to go without Celeste.

He thought of her again, of the way those dark eyes closed slightly as she came, and the way her mouth parted in sweet, delicious abandon...and his body tensed, his erection pushed forward as though trying to get inside of the woman in his mind, and his hips jerked in orgasm.

By the time he returned to the kitchen, Nan was rinsing her bowl in the sink. "Obviously, your idea of a quick shower and mine aren't the same. I assumed you decided to rest for a while so I put your gumbo in the fridge, but I can heat it up if you want."

"No, thanks," he said. Unfortunately, even after his climax, he was still only hungry for one thing. Celeste. Her touch. Her smile.

Her kiss.

He sat at the table and reached for the stack of letters in the center. More than anything else he'd done today, he'd read and reread the letters from the attic. He was convinced that he'd missed something. His grandmother had said that he and Nanette would find what they needed in the attic. While Dax knew that the letters would help Nanette with her quest for historical-landmark status if she ever decided to share them with the world, he hadn't found anything that would help him get Celeste back.

"Still hoping to find something?" she asked, drying her hands on a towel, then sitting next to him at the table.

She peered over his shoulder at the letter in his hand and frowned. "I still don't want to show them to anyone. Maybe we won't have to."

"Maybe not," Dax said. "I do think this is what she intended for you to use, whether you choose to or not. But she said what you *and* I needed was in the attic. I know she was talking about these letters."

"Maybe she wasn't talking about you getting Celeste back. Maybe all she was talking about was the historical landmark status, and she said both of our names because we're the ones who've been doing the most to try to find proof."

Dax didn't buy that. His grandmother had said that what Nan *and* Dax wanted was in the attic. She knew what Nan wanted, to prove the house was inhabited back then, and Adeline Vicknair undoubtedly knew what Dax wanted too.

"No. She included me because of Celeste. I know it. I've just got to figure out how to use these letters to help me learn where she is, and why she can't remember what happens when she's there."

They continued to scan the letters. He nearly knew them all by heart now, and there was nothing in them that referred to spirits stuck in the middle. Every ghost his great-great-great-great-grandmother mentioned was simply another assignment needing a little help to find the light.

"Have you been back up to the attic?" she asked.

Dax shook his head. "No, why?"

"Maybe you're right. The letters are what I need if I decide to turn them over to the historical society—which I won't," she said. "But maybe there's something else in the attic intended for you. I mean, you pretty much stopped searching when you found the letters, didn't you? Maybe there's another clue up there that would help you find Celeste. Or whatever you need may have been in the stuff that Monique and Ryan took."

"No, I thought of that. They'd already cleaned out what they wanted before I got the note from Grandma Adeline. She knew what was up there, and she knew that what I needed was there."

"Okay, so it's still there. Don't you think if it were in these letters, we'd have found it?"

Dax looked at her green eyes, alive with excitement.

She stood, grabbing his arm. "Come on. If you're not going to eat anyway, there's no reason for us to sit around in the kitchen when we could be looking for whatever you're supposed to find in the attic. Plus, now I'm curious. Let's go check it out."

He dropped the letter he was perusing on top of the stack. "I know it's a long shot, but you could be right. I did stop looking when I found these."

"Exactly." Suddenly quite energetic for a woman who'd been teaching ninth-graders all day, she led the way to the third floor, taking the steps two at a time.

When they reached the attic access, she moved to the side. "You'll have to pull the string. I can't reach it." She pointed to the thin rope hanging from the panel in the ceiling.

He grabbed it and pulled. Same as the last time, Dax barely made it out of the way of the unfolding ladder before it slammed him in the face. He caught the lower portion just before it hit the hardwood. Several dents and crevices already marred the floor from where previous Vicknairs hadn't been so careful.

"Ladies first." He waved Nanette up the ladder.

"Well, I'll be, we do have a gentleman in the family after all." She started up, with Dax close behind.

"Hell, I'm just letting you go first because it's dark up there," he said, then laughed when she shoved a foot toward his head.

"Smart-ass."

They emerged into the dusty room, and Nan quickly located the pull-string to turn on the room's single bulb.

"I thought you covered that back up before we left the other day," she said, pointing to the chifforobe, which was the only piece of furniture in the room that wasn't covered by a sheet or plastic.

"I did." Dax moved toward the large piece of furniture.

"Did it slide off?" she asked, and then located the sheet, folded in a perfect square. "I—guess not."

"Didn't I put it back on?" he asked, but he *knew* that he had.

"Even if you didn't, you tossed all of the sheets aside when you were looking through the furniture. I remember. And that sheet wasn't tossed, it's been folded. Neatly." She paused, leaned down and touched the corner of the white cloth. "As neat as Grandma Adeline always folded things, I'd say."

Feeling a slight kick of adrenaline at the hint that there was still something to find, Dax pulled the top drawer open and slid his hand inside. It was completely empty. "There's something else here," he said, knowing their grandmother was trying to help him. "We've just got to find it."

Nanette opened the long door that composed one side of the piece and started rummaging through several old quilts and blankets. "I agree. She wants us to find something else, but what?"

All of the drawers had previously been stuffed with cards and letters, but Dax had removed them. Even so, he pulled open the next drawer and slid his hand inside, but again came up empty.

"Find anything?" he asked as Nanette removed the last of the quilts and placed it on the floor beside her. She ran her hands along the wooden bottom and up the sides.

"I thought perhaps there was some sort of hiding place in here. I don't know, like maybe a secret panel or something," she said. "But I can't find anything."

Dax looked down at her, still in the dress pants she'd worn to school, crouched on the dirty floor, running her hands across dusty old wood trying to find a secret panel. Her black hair had something grayish on one side, and he'd bet that it was probably a cobweb.

He laughed. He couldn't help it. Here Nan was, the

girl in the family who always tried to portray herself as the oldest, the toughest and the biggest hard-ass when it came to dealing with spirits and sticking to the rules, but every now and then, Nanette's softer side made an appearance, and right now was one of those times.

"What are you laughing at?" she asked, raising one curved black brow as she spoke.

"You, looking for a secret panel. You expecting to find a lion and a witch in there?"

She laughed loudly. "You never know."

"And then there's that cobweb in your hair. I only wish I had a camera."

She ran her hands through her hair, captured the web, then flicked it from her fingers. "Disgusting."

"That's exactly what I was thinking." He leaned down and touched her shoulder. "But I really appreciate you helping me, Nan."

She smiled. "No problem."

Then a loud *thunk* echoed from the chifforobe, and both of them jerked toward the sound.

"You hear that?" she asked.

"Yeah, where'd it come from?"

She leaned back into the elongated area that had held the quilts and blankets. "I think, maybe, in here?" She ran her hands around the interior again, but shook her head as she apparently found nothing different.

Dax had surveyed all of the drawers except the bottom one. He pulled on it, and it stuck. He yanked on the drawer again, and this time it came free.

Nanette leaned over him, and her shadow made it impossible for him to see inside, so he slid his hand against the bottom to make sure he hadn't missed anything before. He didn't anticipate finding anything, though, since he distinctly remembered doing the same thing when he'd originally found the letters.

However, as he reached toward the back of the deep drawer, he realized that it felt different; the back wasn't wooden like the rest of the drawer's interior. No, this was some kind of fabric covering, and Dax was surprised he hadn't noticed it before.

"Hold on, I've got something," he said, moving his hand over the fabric until he found its edge. He realized that this wasn't merely cloth covering the back of the drawer; it was something lying flush against it. He maneuvered his fingers into the tiny crack between the fabric edge and the wooden side, and then pulled it to remove…a book.

Nan backed up to let the limited light hit the object, and the two of them stared at the tattered book in Dax's hands. The outer covering was a rose-colored cloth, and in the center, embroidered in swirling script and oddly similar to their grandmother's handwriting, were three words.

Until You Return.

Dax opened the book, tilted it to catch the light and read aloud, "'May 1, 1863. My darling John-Paul, keeping the Vicknair secrets about the beloved spirits is a duty I willingly chose upon becoming your wife. However, I never knew that I would also have to keep your visits a secret. For two years I dreamed of being with you again as a wife needs to be with her husband, and for the past two weeks I have been, nearly every night. This house has been so lonely with you at war, and my soul is waning from the many soldier spirits I am called to help find the light. Being with you that way again makes it bearable. I only wish we knew how you get through, and how we could lengthen your stays. I miss you so when you're gone, John-Paul.'"

"John-Paul," Nanette repeated. "That's her husband, and in 1863, he'd have still been fighting in the war."

"But he was visiting her. Or rather, his spirit was visiting," Dax said, his blood pumping fiercely. "This is it, Nan." He squinted to see the writing, faint on the weathered page, and moved it toward the light. "Damn, I can barely see the rest of this."

"Come on, let's take it downstairs to a better light." Nan crossed the room and quickly descended the ladder, and Dax followed.

"In here," he said when they neared the second-floor sitting room.

The two of them entered the room, but instead of finding the place vacant, they found Ryan and Monique, huddled together on the settee, staring at the tea service.

"Ryan's waiting on his first ghost!" Monique exclaimed. "He came home from work and said that he'd been hearing hammers and saws all day long, but not the ones that were surrounding him at his roofing job. That's when it hit me. Now that we're married, he'll start getting ghosts too." She squeezed her husband and smiled broadly. "And I wanted to be with him when he gets the first one."

"Hammers and saws?" Nan asked.

"I'm assuming he may get spirits who are injured in construction accidents, or something like that, don't you think? That would make sense, wouldn't it?" Monique asked.

"I guess it would," Nan said.

"Who'd have thought—a few months ago, I was the ghost needing help, and now I'm going to be the one on the other end?" Ryan kissed Monique softly.

"Hey, what have you got?" Monique asked, leaning forward to steal a peek at the book in Dax's hand.

"Maybe a way to get Celeste back," Nanette said.

And at Monique's shocked expression, Dax added, "I'll tell you about it later, sis. Right now, I have to read this. Good luck with your first assignment, Ryan."

"Thanks."

Nanette and Dax turned and started down the stairs.

"Ryan's a medium now," she whispered. "I hadn't even realized…"

"That our spouses will become mediums by marriage?" Dax questioned. "Neither did I. I mean, I never thought about it, but our parents were all mediums. And obviously—" he held up the book "—Clara Vicknair was a medium by marriage."

"I know. I just hadn't thought about it in terms of my future husband being a medium, but it does make sense." When they reached the foyer, she went straight to the front door and opened it. "The porch. It'll be quiet out here, and the lighting outside will help us see the writing better."

Dax followed her, then dropped into a rocker and flipped the book open, while Nanette scooted another rocker near enough to see.

They scanned the next few pages and learned that John-Paul had visited Clara yet again two days later, then again three days after that. Through all of the daily entries, Clara discussed the war, and particularly the raid she'd heard about, a raid on Vicksburg.

"How sad," Nanette whispered.

"What?"

"That so many lives were lost then. Read this one." She pointed to the opposite page from the one Dax was scanning, and he turned his attention to the curling script.

"'My darling John-Paul, I had twelve more ghosts from the Vicksburg raid, some Confederate, some Union, and all of them needing help through. Most wanted to see their newborn babes before they crossed. Oh, to conceive from our visits now, but I know that isn't possible. Even so, when you come back, I'll give you a child, a baby, with hair dark and wavy like yours, and definitely with your vivid green eyes, and perhaps my smile.'"

"Twelve soldiers in one day," Nanette said, emotion filling her tone. "Bless their hearts, and bless her heart for helping them."

Dax nodded, and flipped through the pages, passing several days where the entries were virtually the same—

Clara helping several ghosts, and John-Paul visiting as often as he could to be with his wife. But she continually mentioned that her husband never knew when he was coming, or how long he could stay.

Just like Celeste.

"Do you think they ever figured out how he visited? Or—was he dead?" he asked, then said, "But that wouldn't be possible, would it? I mean, the Vicknair line didn't stop with him, so they had to have had a child together."

"Not necessarily," Nan corrected. "There were several Vicknair brothers who fought for the Confederates, though he was probably the only one whose wife stayed here during the war. All of the records I found said that most women returned to their parents' homes when their husbands left for the war. I'm guessing Clara stayed behind to help the spirits, or she'd have done the same. Anyway, one of the others could have had children."

"Didn't you bring home that information from the parish courthouse? Or copies of it?"

Nan jumped up from her rocker. "Yeah, it's in my room." She darted inside the house, while Dax flipped through more of Clara's diary and hoped to find a hint as to whether John-Paul was alive or dead, and whether he'd ever made it back to her in his physical form.

A single line in all capital letters, the text written jerkily, as though Clara had been upset at the time, caught Dax's attention.

MY DARLING, DON'T COME BACK.

Dax read aloud, "'My darling John-Paul, another

soldier came today. As my duty, I helped him see his young wife and find the light, but this soldier knew things, things about you. Your visits weaken you, my darling, and this soldier knew that your body is already weak, wounded at Vicksburg. He said your body is in a hospital, and that you're dying, John-Paul. You're dying! Oh, darling, don't you see? Your visits are only achievable because your spirit is wavering, deciding whether to yield to the light or to stay. Please, John-Paul, please do not allow your spirit to return. Wait, my darling. Heal, and then return to me, alive and well. Let your spirit rest, and join your body once more. Then return to me, forever. Return to me, whole. I would not have merely a part of you, my dearest John-Paul. I need all of you.'"

Dax turned the page, but there weren't any additional entries.

The front door opened and Nanette bounded through, holding a sheet of paper. "Dax, they thought he was dead. They even reported him dead at one point, had him listed in the fatalities from the Vicksburg raid, but he wasn't dead. He was injured. Dying. And then he returned home. He came back to her."

"But she nearly lost him, because he grew weaker every time he visited her in spirit. His spirit was trying to determine whether to live or die, and she almost lost him, because his spirit wanted to be with her again, before he crossed over." Dax handed the diary to Nan. "Celeste isn't dead, Nanette. She's dying."

15

DAX PRESSED HIS FOOT on the accelerator and the Beemer instantly responded, shooting forward on Highway 90 in a direct path to Houma. He withdrew his cell phone and pressed the Send key to redial Chloe's parents. He'd left three messages but hadn't heard from them yet. They'd know what happened to Celeste. He'd have asked them before now if he'd only realized that Celeste wasn't dead. She'd been in the same accident that took their daughter's life; surely they could tell him what had happened to her.

Thank goodness he knew them well enough to ask, after spending that week with them at the beach this summer in order to help Chloe communicate with them before she crossed. That week was one of the best of his life, not only because he'd helped Chloe see the beach for the first time with her parents, but because Celeste had been there too.

Maybe when she'd made the decision to stay behind and help Chloe cross, she had in fact kept her body from surrendering its spirit completely. He'd never even considered that possibility, didn't know it was an option. But now he knew, and he had to find out where she was, how she was and how he could get to her.

Celeste was hurt, but how badly hurt, Dax didn't know. What he did know—thanks to Clara Vicknair's diary—was that every time she visited him, she weakened her physical body and therefore lessened her chances to stay on this side. What if that last visit had caused her to cross completely?

He thanked God that there was hardly any traffic. Holding his cell phone to his ear, he didn't hear anything. No ringing, no voice message, nothing. He glanced at the call screen, and saw he had no service. He tossed it to the passenger's seat.

"Come on!" Gripping the steering wheel tighter, he wished Houma were closer than an hour and a half from the Vicknair plantation. Then again, thanks to driving like a madman, he'd be there soon. However, even when he got to the city where the bus had crashed, would he be able to find her? Would she be in a hospital in Houma, or would they have taken her to one of the New Orleans hospitals? Or would she have been transported somewhere else? That was entirely possible. She could have been transferred to the nearest facility that was best equipped to handle her injuries.

Her injuries. She had been hurt badly enough to keep her in the middle realm for four months.

Four months.

And he was solely responsible for making her worse.

"Say I didn't hurt her," he said, and tried to decide which hospital to go to first. There were two in Houma, the Leonard J. Chabert Medical Center and the Terrebonne General Medical Center. If he didn't get in touch with Chloe's folks before he hit the city limits, he'd simply drive to one, then the other, and see if Celeste was at either of them.

He had a few Houma doctors on his pharmaceutical route; he'd visited them just last week. What if he'd been on one floor of the hospital, and she was on another? And how many times had he visited these hospitals over the past four months? Was she there all that time? Could he have seen her? Helped her?

That bus wreck had occurred on the Fourth of July. So long ago.

His cell phone rang, and he quickly picked it up. "Hello?"

"Did you find her yet?" Nanette asked.

"No. I'm not even sure where she is. I haven't been able to get in touch with Chloe's family, but I'm about a mile from one of the hospitals in Houma, and I'm going to see if she's there."

"I checked the Internet to see if I could find any information about the accident, thinking that maybe some of the news articles might have said where they took the people who were injured."

"And?" Dax reached the entrance to Terrebonne General Medical Center and pulled in.

"Nothing. The newspaper articles list the number of fatalities and casualties, but no names or specifics. Sorry, Dax."

"That's okay. I appreciate you trying. Listen, I'm at

the first hospital. I'm going to see if she's here." He parked the car, got out and sprinted toward the entrance.

"Call me and let me know when you find her. I'm going to keep searching the Net."

"Okay." He disconnected and entered the hospital lobby.

An elderly woman in a pink hospital smock sat behind the information desk and smiled at him when he neared.

"Can I help you locate a patient?" she asked.

"Yes. Celeste Beauchamp."

"Beauchamp," she repeated softly as her arthritic fingers clicked the keys of the computer in front of her. Then she shook her head and frowned. "I'm so sorry. There's no patient here by that name. Could she be listed under a different name, perhaps?"

"No, thanks." Frustrated, he turned and headed out. As he got into his car, his cell phone started up again. Nanette was impatient. He punched the Send key. "She wasn't there."

"Excuse me?" the man said on the other end. "Is this Dax Vicknair?"

"Yes, yes, it is," Dax said, easily recognizing Chloe's father's voice. "Mr. Reynolds?"

"I'm afraid I just got your message. Is—well, is anything wrong? I had to wonder if this has anything to do with Chloe. We've sensed her lately, both of us have, but we thought it was because of her birthday last week. She'd have been seven, you know. We think she came to see us then, or was watching us, or however it works.

But everything's okay with her, isn't it? I mean, she crossed fine, like you said, didn't she?"

"Yes." He shouldn't have left such a vague message, Dax now realized. He sure didn't want to cause the Reynolds family to worry about their daughter, but he simply hadn't been thinking about anything but Celeste when he called. "I haven't heard from Chloe since she crossed over, but I know that she crossed fine," he reassured. Celeste had told him that she'd personally seen Chloe enter the light, so he had no doubt that their daughter was safe and sound on the other side, unlike Celeste, hovering in the middle. "And I don't doubt that you're sensing her presence," he added. "Spirits do tend to keep an eye on their loved ones on this side, until they see you again over there."

Chloe's father sighed heavily. "Well, that's a relief." His voice grew faint as he turned away from the phone. "She's okay, dear."

"Sorry to have alarmed you," Dax said, "but I believe you can help me with another spirit, or individual, I should say. A woman who was on the bus with Chloe that day. Her name was—is—Celeste Beauchamp."

"The counselor for the camp?"

"Yes," Dax said quickly, thankful that Mr. Reynolds readily recognized her name. That was a good sign, wasn't it? "The counselor. Do you know what happened to her? Or where she is now?"

"I know that she didn't stay here long. I mean, in Louisiana. She was in one of the local hospitals for a while, but then, when there wasn't any change, her family wanted to take her back home. We get updates on her condition, though, through the church bulletin, she's on the prayer list. Hold on, and I'll get it."

"Wait!" Dax said, but Reynolds had already put the phone down. Celeste's parents wanted to take her back home? Where was home?

Dax felt like kicking himself—he'd never even considered that she wasn't from Houma. That was where the campers were from, but Celeste wasn't a camper; she was a counselor. Why hadn't he ever asked her where she lived?

He recalled her telling him that the first time she'd tried a muffuletta was the day of the bus crash. He should have put it together then—she hadn't had the traditional New Orleans sandwich before because she wasn't from Louisiana. And there were her comments about poinsettias not being able to grow outside her parents' house…

Why hadn't he put it together?

"Okay, I've got it now," Mr. Reynolds said. "Celeste Beauchamp *is* still listed on our prayer list. She's been on it since the summer. Let's see…she's at Parkridge Medical Center in Chattanooga, Tennessee. Room 302."

Chattanooga. Near the Smoky Mountains, definitely not a place where poinsettias would survive outside. "Can you tell me about her condition?" Dax asked, scrawling the name of the hospital and room number on a notepad and struggling to keep his voice calm in spite of the way his mind was currently reeling. How was she? And how quickly could he get to her?

"I assume she's still in a coma," Mr. Reynolds said bluntly. "From what we heard, the doctors couldn't find any reason for her not to wake up, and a few times we got reports that she seemed to be getting better, but evidently, she didn't come completely out of it, or she slipped back into it, or however it works. Last week, though, at church, they announced that her condition had worsened. I'm not sure how, they just asked for more prayers."

Her condition had worsened. Because of Dax.

"Room 302, you said?" Dax asked, starting his car. He needed to get to Chattanooga as quickly as possible.

"Yeah. Parkridge Medical Center," Mr. Reynolds repeated. "You going to see her? Are you supposed to help her cross?"

"No," Dax said. "I'm not supposed to help her cross—" or he sure hoped he wasn't "—but I am going to see her."

"Well, I hope everything goes okay," he said. "Let us know how she's doing."

"I will," Dax promised, then said goodbye and hung up the phone. Without taking time to second-guess his decision, he pulled out of the hospital parking lot and started toward New Orleans International. If he pushed it, he could be there in forty minutes. Celeste's life was at stake. Her condition was worsening. What did that mean? And who was with her? Surely she wasn't alone. Her family would be there, right? Her mother, father and sister. They'd be with her, trying to coax her out of the coma.

He dialed information for the airport numbers. He'd get on the first flight out, to Chattanooga, and to Celeste.

Within fifteen minutes, he'd booked his ticket and had his car soaring in a beeline for the New Orleans airport. He had just enough time to get to the airport, park his car and run to the plane. Security would normally slow him down, but without any luggage or carry-on items, he could make it. He had to get to her before she went to the other side.

Failure wasn't an option.

16

"PLEASE MAKE SURE your seat is in the upright position and that your seat belt is securely fastened as we prepare for our descent." The flight attendant's voice echoed through the cabin.

Dax placed a hand against the cool glass of the window and stared out at the city. Even in the darkness, he could see the dark shadows of mountains surrounding Chattanooga and the grayish clouds that cloaked them all. Smoky Mountains they were called; now he saw why.

A loud click through the PA was followed by the attendant's voice again. "Local time is 6:30 p.m., and the current temperature is twenty-eight degrees."

Twenty-eight degrees. Louisiana had been in the mid-seventies. No wonder Celeste had said she didn't think poinsettias would grow outside. If he'd paid attention, he might have realized that she came from a state with mountains, and cold weather, and probably snow. Definitely not a place where ten-foot poinsettias blanketed the side of a house.

But she'd loved those poinsettias; she'd loved the plantation. If Dax got there in time, and she woke up in the land of the living instead of crossing over, would she want to go back there, with him? And would she want to do more than merely visit?

Would she stay forever?

He thought of those dark eyes, and the way they'd looked when he'd told her he loved her. She didn't get a chance to respond, but Dax had known she would've told him that she felt the same. He could see Celeste beside him, the way Ryan was beside Monique earlier, waiting to receive *her* first spirit assignment as Celeste Vicknair. She'd get child spirits, like he did, Dax knew. She was good with children. He could see her teaching at one of the local schools, like Nanette, but with younger children. Kindergarten, or first grade. She'd teach the living, and help the ones who'd lost their lives to find their way to their new homes. And the kids would love her, and Dax would love her…always.

If he could keep her on this side.

He exited the plane and darted through the airport, following the signs to the taxis. Then he barreled outside and got in line with a dozen other people who were bundled from head to toe in hats, scarves, gloves, wool coats and boots. They looked at Dax, in his LSU short-sleeved T-shirt and worn jeans, as though he'd lost his mind. And as his body shuddered in the cold, he realized that they were probably right; he'd lost his mind *and* his heart over Celeste Beauchamp.

"Son, are you okay?" an older man in front of him asked. "Do you—well, do you not own a coat?"

Dax could literally feel the adrenaline pumping through him, the excitement of being this close to Celeste. He'd be with her soon. He was shaking all over—his body's natural response to the sudden jolt in temperature and his lack of proper clothing—but part of that shivering was due to the sheer shock of realizing that she wasn't dead, and from hoping that he'd have a chance to keep her from being that way.

"I didn't pack my coat," he said honestly, his teeth chattering slightly as he spoke. "I didn't pack anything. The woman I love was in an accident, and I'm trying to get to her. She's at Parkridge Medical Center."

"Goodness, why didn't you say so?" a woman said at the front of the line. There were no cabs at the curb yet, but one was pulling up, and she hurriedly waved him forward. The driver got out and walked toward her, but she shook her head. "Take him." She pointed to Dax. "It's an emergency. He needs to get to Parkridge Medical."

All of the people in front of Dax nodded their heads approvingly and even patted his back as he moved past them toward the waiting cab. "Good luck, son," the old man called, and the remainder of the group echoed his sentiment as Dax climbed in.

"Thanks," he said, his heart filled with emotion, not only for the woman he loved, but for the people so willing to help him get to her.

"Parkridge Medical Center?" the driver asked.

"Yes. Can you tell me how far that is from here? How long will it take us to get there?"

"Fifteen minutes," he said, then he turned up the heat in the car. "You're going to freeze here."

"Yeah, I know."

Fifteen minutes until he was with Celeste. Dax leaned his head back against the seat, closed his eyes and thanked the powers that be for giving him this chance.

And that's when he heard it. Faint, but distinct non-etheless. A laugh, no, a giggle. The giggle of a young child. A boy. It'd been a while since he'd had a boy spirit for an assignment; the majority of the children he'd helped lately were girls, but this was most definitely a boy, and while Dax listened, that giggle became louder, as though the child was getting closer...

"No."

"Something wrong?" the cabbie asked from the front seat, his brown eyes surveying Dax from the mirror. "You're not the carsick type, are you? Because we're nearly there."

"No. I—I just need to make a call. I forgot something, or rather, I forgot about something, at home." He withdrew his cell phone from his pocket and quickly dialed the plantation.

Nanette answered on the first ring. "Dax? Are you there? Have you seen her?"

He'd called her from the airport and let her know about Celeste. "Yeah, I'm in Chattanooga, but I'm not at the hospital yet, and I need you to check on something for me."

The cabbie relayed, "Five more minutes."

"We're five minutes from the hospital now, but I've got a problem."

"What is it?"

Dax didn't want to blurt out that he had a ghost on the way, not in front of the cabdriver who seemed to have taken an acute interest in their conversation. Dax could see the guy's lifted brows in the mirror. "I need you to go to the sitting room and check the tea service for me. I think I may have—left something there."

The cabbie's brows furrowed, but he didn't comment. Nanette, however, did.

"No—you've got an assignment?"

"On the way," Dax said. "I don't think it'll be there yet, but it's coming."

Nan's breathing quickened on the other end, and he could hear the sound of her footsteps, as though she was running up the stairs. "Hang on. I'm checking."

"I usually have a day, but this one seems pretty near, like I might not have so long this time."

"I'm in here now, Dax. Nothing on the tea service yet. What are you going to do? You know you have to come home if you get an assignment. There's no telling what the powers that be will do if you don't. They don't like to wait."

"I know." Dax had once been on the other side of the state on a pharmaceutical route when an assignment was delivered, and by the time he made it home, the voices in his head had been so loud, children squealing and screaming and yelling and laughing, that he nearly couldn't drive. And this time he was three states away. "But I'm not leaving until I see her, Nanette, no matter what."

"Attaboy," the driver said, stopping the cab in front of the entrance to Parkridge Medical Center.

Dax reached for his wallet, but the guy shook his head. "This one's on me. You go get the girl."

"I agree with him," Nanette said, evidently hearing the cabbie. "You do what you've got to do there. Take care of Celeste, and I'll watch for your assignment on the tea service. When it comes, I'll call you and let you know."

Dax smiled. It wasn't like Nanette to forgo rules, particularly when they had to do with the spirits, but whether she admitted it or not, she had a soft spot for love, and she knew Dax's love was in this hospital. "Thanks, Nan."

"Just let me know how things go there, and I'll do the same from here. Good luck, Dax." She hung up.

Dax sprinted through the hospital lobby to the elevators and punched the button. Within seconds, he stepped off at the third floor. A nurses' station was directly in front of the elevator, and Dax took advantage of one of the nurses looking his way. "Room 302?"

She pointed to one of the hallways that branched away from the station. "Second room on your right."

Dax hurried to the room, opened the door without knocking—and saw her. She was on the bed, her eyes closed and her long blond curls draped over the pillow. The top of her blouse, the same sage green blouse she'd been wearing when she came to him, was visible above the sheet.

A young woman sat beside the bed and held Celeste's hand. She looked up at him, and though her eyes were bloodshot and tired, her face was vaguely similar to Celeste's. Her hair was more sandy than blond, and in a style that Dax would classify as stylishly modern.

"Nelsa?"

She blinked, then nodded. "Do I know you?" she asked. "Or—does she?" She looked at her sister, then leaned over her and kissed her cheek.

"Yes," he said, stepping toward the bed. He wanted to run to Celeste, to hold her, to beg her to wake up and be with him on *this* side. But how could he tell Nelsa that he was Celeste's lover when he hadn't even been to the hospital since she'd been hurt?

Dax's head reeled. What to say to make this woman, hovering protectively over her sister, let him get near?

"Excuse me?"

Dax turned toward the woman's voice behind him and saw an older couple with cups of coffee cradled in their hands and confused looks on their faces. The woman looked as if she hadn't slept in weeks, or more probably, months. Her eyes were puffy and swollen, and her skin was void of color; she looked as though she'd been through hell. Then again, she'd been through the closest thing to it, the scare of losing a child. The man beside her wasn't overly tall, but he was stoutly built and had a disapproving scowl on his face. "Who are you?" he asked. "And what are you doing here?"

Celeste's parents.

No doubt a stranger showing up in their daughter's room would make them suspicious, but Dax wasn't a stranger, yet he didn't know how to tell them that.

"I'm a—friend of Celeste's," he started, then shook his head. "No, it's more than that," he said, not willing to lie to Celeste's family. "I love her."

The woman dropped her coffee, and it splattered against her feet on the floor.

"Son, what are you saying? We—we don't even know you," Celeste's father said, then he turned to his wife. "Marian, are you all right?"

"It's him," she whispered, her trembling hand moving to her heart. "You're Dax, aren't you?"

The man's look of irritation swiftly converted to one of shock, and Nelsa stood beside the bed. "Are you? Are you Dax?"

Dax was thrown. How could they know him? But he nodded. "I am."

"She's been calling for you," Nelsa explained. "In fact, your name is the *only* name she's said the whole time. All these months. Dax. We—we didn't know where you were, didn't know *who* you were, and we tried to find you but didn't know where to look."

She'd been calling his name? Dax's pulse beat wildly. If she'd been calling his name on this side, that meant that—what?—her spirit had been back here and trying to merge? That she remembered him on this side as well? Or was he just grasping at straws? Would her spirit come back to her body, the way John-Paul's had?

Or had Dax ruined her chance for that when he'd kept her with him for so long?

"Where have you been?" her mother asked. "If you love her, where have you been?" She took a shaky breath. "I—we—didn't even know about you, had no idea. And I'd have thought if you knew her, and you loved her, you would have come shortly after the accident. But you didn't come." She shook her head. "Why not?"

"I've been in Louisiana, where I live. I didn't know that she was here. I just found out today, and I came as soon as I heard." He had to concentrate on his words now, because the little boy's giggles were returning, and they were louder, much louder.

The machine beside the bed began to beep, and they all turned toward it.

"No." Nelsa grabbed the call button and pressed it rapidly. "It's dropping again!"

The little boy's laughter throbbed in Dax's mind, and he had no doubt his spirit was nearly ready to come to the plantation, if he wasn't already there. "What's dropping?" he asked, stepping toward the bed, and Celeste.

"Her heart rate. Just like it did those other three times. And the doctor said she wouldn't make it if she went through one of those episodes again," Nelsa said. She turned to Dax. "She's been wanting you, and now you're here, but she's leaving us!"

"No, Celeste," Marian Beauchamp pleaded, moving quickly to the bed and grabbing Celeste's other hand. "Stay with us, honey. Please!"

Dax's ghost was nearly there, the laughter so loud, so intense, that he barely heard Nelsa, even though she was screaming too. And then he realized what she'd said. Those other three times. Celeste's heart rate had faltered before, and Dax knew when—when she came to him, to help his spirits cross. And now he had another spirit coming, and she was fading.

"No!" Dax yelled, but his voice merely joined the other panicked ones in the room…and the laughter in his head grew so overwhelming that he gripped the bedrail to stay upright. He knew what was happening, and he didn't know how to stop it. Celeste was trying to get back to him, with the little-boy ghost. But if her spirit succeeded, her body would fail. He'd lose her for good, because she was trying to see him again. "No!"

17

CELESTE'S MOUTH was dry, her head throbbed and every ounce of her being violently protested any movement, but she wasn't going to stop. She couldn't.

Because she was so, so close.

The thick darkness surrounding her grew less dense with every step, and she could almost see some form of light in the distance. She braced herself against the wall, her fingers gripping its coolness as she inched her way forward. Another step, rest, concentrate. Two more steps, stop, rest, concentrate. She could get back there. Stopping was not an option. This was the only way to Dax, and she wasn't going to let her exhaustion keep her from getting to him again.

She could hear voices from both sides. Voices behind her, from that pathway where she'd heard them before, were once again calling her name. Someone screamed, and someone cried.

"Celeste!" they yelled. "Please, Celeste!"

"No," she whispered. There wasn't any way she would give up now. She could see the opening that led to that room in the middle, and it wasn't dark now. In fact, it was a faint yellow. And she heard voices from the middle too, but those voices were different. One was a woman. Adeline, perhaps? Or was it someone else?

Celeste paused to rest again, tuned out the voices behind her and focused on what the woman was saying.

"*Chère*, it's going to be okay," Adeline said, her voice a little higher than usual, as though she were talking to a child. "Don't worry, Ike, my Dax will take care of you."

Dax. Someone—Ike—was going to see Dax, and Adeline was about to send him through.

"W-wait," Celeste said, but her voice was so weak that it barely formed a whisper.

Did Adeline hear her?

"Sure, *chère*, you can tell your mama and daddy bye. I know they'd like that, and that they'll want to know that you'll be okay. Dax will help you do that, and you'll like him, but if you don't mind, I'd like for you to visit with me for a little while before you go. My Dax is taking care of something right now, and he knows you want to see him, but he needs to see a—a friend of his before he goes back home. I can show you some really nice things while we're waiting for him."

Thunder roared in the distance, and Celeste heard Adeline again, her voice a bit worried as she spoke to the boy. "I won't keep you too long, *chère*, and of course, if you want to go on through, you can. I can't stop you, you know."

"What can you show me?" the little boy asked as Celeste licked her lips and tried again.

"Wait, please," she said hoarsely.

The two people in the room ahead of her continued to talk, and she wanted to cry. No, she wanted to scream.

But she couldn't.

Celeste braced her hands against the wall and forced another step, then another. Nearly there. Just a few more. She wasn't going to lose this chance.

"I can show you what the other side of the clouds looks like," Adeline said. "Or we can go hide in the middle of them and watch the planes go by. Would you like that?"

"Cool!" Ike yelled.

"Wait!" Celeste's attempt to scream was so weak it sounded more like a whisper, but thank goodness, the little boy heard her.

"Who's that?" he asked, moving toward Celeste as she entered the middle room, then slumped against the wall.

"Oh, no," Adeline whispered. "Celeste, dear," she said, then she frowned and looked behind her as a loud boom of thunder roared through the room. "I thought you'd gone to rest. You need to go back, *chère*. That's the way to Dax."

The thunder boomed even louder, and the middle wall opened, the light filling its center and warming Celeste's cold spirit.

"I thought *I* was going to Dax." The boy pouted.

"You are, Ike, but remember, I'm going to show you a few things around here first. Dax needs to take care of some things, and he's working on that now."

Celeste blinked, and fought the way the light pulled her toward it. The entire middle wall was open and glowing and beckoning her now, but Dax wasn't there. "I want to go with you," she whispered to the boy. "To see Dax." Then she looked at Adeline. "Let us through."

"You can't go that way again," Adeline said, frowning as she shook her head. "Oh, *chère*, please. You have to trust me this time. The way behind you is the only way for you to go now." She lowered her voice. "It's the right way, *chère*. Please, trust me, I can't tell you more."

Again, booming thunder roared around them, and the light got so warm that Celeste squinted at its radiance.

"This is it, Celeste," Adeline said. "You have a choice, but Dax's way isn't part of your decision anymore. That path is closed to you now, you're too weak for it. And you're not going to be strong enough to go down it again, *chère*."

Celeste looked at the light, and then turned toward the dark path behind her, where those voices were still calling her name. She listened to them, the same voices she'd heard time and time again. Every other time, they'd merely blended in an incomprehensible mix of screams and sobs, with none of them really standing out as unique. But now…

She swallowed, leaned toward the sound. Then she turned back to Adeline. "That's Dax's voice, isn't it? Dax is there? Back there?"

"I'm going to keep Ike company for a while so that

Dax can take care of a few things before he visits. That's all I'm allowed to say, *chère*."

"Dax." Celeste started toward the darkened path, but the light pulled her back, caused her to stumble. She held up a hand and saw that her glow was almost blinding now, and her feet refused to cooperate; they wouldn't move down the path. Instead, she was inching her way backward, toward that vivid, powerful light.

She didn't want to go. But she was too tired to fight it.

"Help me," she whispered, reaching out to Dax's voice.

18

"MAMA, LOOK! It's lower than before!" Horrified, Nelsa pointed to the monitor beside the bed. "We have to get someone!" She ran out of the room with her mother close at her heels.

"Hold on, baby," Marian pleaded before she left. "We're getting the doctors. Don't you dare leave us!"

Her husband moved to one side of the bed and grabbed his daughter's hand, and Dax, still fighting the little boy's laughter in his head, gripped the bedrail in a determined effort to fight the pull of the little spirit. No way would he leave her now, and he prayed she wasn't going to leave him…for good.

"She's wanted you. Let her know you're here," Mr. Beauchamp demanded. "She hasn't come to us. Maybe she'll come to you."

Dax gazed down at the woman he loved, and listened to the beats of her heart growing fainter. He blinked past the pounding in his head and said the words he'd only spoken once before.

"Celeste, I love you. Please, come back to me, *chère*. I'm here. Don't—" He didn't look up at Mr. Beauchamp to see his reaction, but simply forged on with what he believed she needed to hear. "Don't try to get to me the other way, *chère*. I'm here. On this side. Don't you dare cross without me."

"No!" her father cried, and Dax heard the beeps growing further apart, at the same time that the little boy's laughter got even stronger.

They were losing her because she was trying to go to him, trying to go the other way, to the Vicknair plantation. And if she did…

"Celeste!" Dax yelled fiercely. "Don't leave me, *chère*, please. I don't want to live without you."

"Dear God!" Her father shook his head in denial. "No! Somebody help! Dammit, where is her doctor?"

Dax's tears fell upon Celeste's cheeks. "Don't leave me."

"In here!" Nelsa ran into the room with her mother and two nurses close behind.

"She's crashing. Get Dr. Pavere," one nurse directed, while the other relayed the information through the intercom by the bed. They quickly took over, with one of them examining the machines hooked to Celeste and the other one checking her pulse. Then a tall, bald man with glasses and a stethoscope rushed in.

"We need the room cleared," he said briskly, stepping around one of the nurses to get to Celeste.

The nurse turned toward all of them, hovering helplessly around the bed. "I'm sorry. We need you to step into the hall."

Nelsa wrapped an arm around her crying mother and ushered her out, while her father followed, but Dax stood-stock still, unable to leave her now that he'd found her.

"No," he said. "She can't die now."

Amazingly, at that very moment, the little boy's laughter grew softer, so faint, in fact, that Dax barely heard it at all.

"I'm sorry," the nurse said, placing her hand on Dax's arm and effectively turning him around toward the door. "You *have* to wait in the hall."

"No! Celeste, this way! I'm here, *chère!*" He turned, pushed past the nurse and forced his way to the bed. Then he did something he'd never done before; he brought his hands to her face, and touched the woman he loved, tenderly stroking his own tears from her cheeks. "Don't leave me, *chère.*"

"I'm sorry, but you *have* to leave," the nurse repeated sternly as she reached for Dax and attempted to pull him away.

Dax glared at the woman. "I can't leave her now. I won't."

"Dax."

The voice was barely audible, but Dax heard it, recognized it. He turned sharply and saw the doctor staring disbelievingly at the woman in the bed, her eyes opened and peering…at Dax.

"Do—it again," she said softly.

"Oh, my God," the nurse beside Dax exclaimed.

His tears fell again, but these were tears of joy. She

was back. Here. With him. And the beating of her heart, growing stronger with every second, said she'd stay here this time.

"Do what again, *chère*?"

She licked her lips, then whispered, "Touch."

His laughter rolled out, and he leaned over her, cradled her face within his hands and smiled.

"Go get her family," the doctor instructed the nurses. "They'll want to see this." He shook his head. "Ms. Beauchamp, I've seen a few miracles in my time—it comes with the territory," he added with a grin. "But this is one for the record books." He looked at Dax. "And it reminds me of the power of love. I'm going to let you have your reunion now, but I'll need to come back later for a few tests, not that I think we're going to find anything wrong, since we were just basically waiting for you to wake up, my dear, but still…"

Celeste nodded slowly, her own tears falling now.

Her parents and sister ran in and embraced Celeste. "It's a miracle!" Nelsa said, crying and laughing and touching Celeste in disbelief.

Her father, however, looked directly at Dax. "Thank you, son."

Celeste stared up at him. "Yes, thank you."

Dax was shocked by her eyes, which were the most vivid moss green. "They're incredible," he whispered.

Celeste smiled. "Thanks." Then she turned to her family on the other side of the bed and saw their baffled expressions, but rather than explaining why Dax was surprised by the color of her eyes, Celeste gave them something else to process. "I love him."

Three sets of eyes, also moss green, all widened and focused on Dax, who grinned as though he'd just been guaranteed happiness for life. And he had.

Her mother stroked her fingertips down Celeste's cheeks, then she looked tearfully at Dax. "You brought our daughter back to us. I don't know how we can ever repay you."

"Say you'll give us your blessing," Dax said. "And we'll call it even."

"Our blessing?" her father asked.

"Yes, sir, because, if she says yes, I plan to marry your daughter."

Celeste beamed, and Nelsa nodded approvingly. "Oh, you're going to fit into this family perfectly," she said. "We're kind of big on romance and happily ever after. Dad asked Mom to marry him after their second date."

"Technically, it was the third, if you count that trip to the fair," Marian clarified, smiling at the memory. "And we've always wanted our daughters to have that kind of love." She looked at Celeste. "I suppose you'd like for us to move back out to the hall for a spell so you and Dax can talk about *something* in private."

Still smiling, Celeste nodded.

"Let's go, David," she said to her husband, then kissed Celeste's cheek.

"Just so you know, if she says yes, then you've got our approval," David Beauchamp said. He turned toward the bed, and though Dax didn't see it, he felt certain that Celeste indicated what her answer would be because the man nodded before leaving with his family.

Dax waited for the door to close, then lowered one of the bed rails and sat beside Celeste. "Celeste Beauchamp," he said, his heart thudding loudly, "Will you marry me?"

"Oh, Dax, yes."

Then he kissed her gently, while his hands tenderly caressed her face, then eased over her body, touching her the way he'd only touched her in his dreams.

The heart monitor began to beat fiercely, her heart rate increasing in rapid proportions as they lengthened the kiss and she moaned her contentment.

"Um, oh!"

Dax broke the kiss and turned toward the nurse in the doorway.

"I'm s-sorry," she stuttered, "but her heart rate was going up so quickly that I thought something might be wrong." She giggled. "But I see now that nothing's wrong at all." She turned and left.

Celeste grinned. "How about a Christmas wedding?"

Christmas was just four weeks away, and Dax loved the idea wholeheartedly. He finally had Celeste, the woman he wanted more than life, and he didn't want to waste any time in sharing his name, sharing his life, sharing his heritage. "A Christmas wedding would be perfect," he said.

Her brows furrowed slightly, and she sighed regret-fully. "You need to go help Ike now."

"Ike?"

"A little-boy spirit, coming to see you. He said he'd wait, but he wants to see his parents," she explained. "And he actually pushed me down the pathway to get me here," she said with a smile. "Well, he and your grandmother."

"They pushed you?"

She nodded. "The light was strong, and they knew I needed help."

"I'll make sure to thank Ike then. And I will go help him cross, but then I'll come back to take you home."

"Home," she repeated. "To the plantation?"

"If that's what you want." He added, "You know that if you marry a Vicknair, you'll also be expected to help spirits."

Those beautiful moss green eyes were alive with excitement. "I wouldn't have it any other way."

19

CELESTE HAD BEEN in that hospital bed for four months, an extremely long time indeed. However, those four months seemed like nothing compared to the four weeks the two of them had to wait for their wedding.

Typical for Louisiana, the week of Christmas was marked with unseasonably warm weather, perfect for an outdoor event. Celeste's mother had been doubtful when they told her they were going to be married outdoors on Christmas Eve at the Vicknair plantation, but after arriving in the bayou, Marian Beauchamp had quickly learned that December in Louisiana was like April in Tennessee.

The plantation was more breathtaking than Dax had ever seen, definitely the best that it'd been since the hurricane took its toll. Tiny white lights circled the eight porch columns and almost completely disguised the fact that they were still slightly leaning from Katrina's damage. The same type of lights were also mingled through the poinsettia hedges to cast a red glow against the sides of the house.

Nanette had borrowed several huge white tents, traditionally used during the Mardi Gras festivities in

February, from the high school, and guests were currently enjoying champagne beneath their curved roofs, also lit with tiny white lights. The mingling conversations had the same basic theme—the bride was radiant, the ceremony was beautiful and the Vicknair plantation was the perfect setting for such an incredible festivity. Everyone was impressed to see how far the cousins had come toward restoring the place to its original magnificence—except for the parish president, Charles Roussel, of course.

Although Dax tried to persuade Nanette to include John-Paul and Clara Vicknair's letters with the nomination packet she sent to the state historic preservation officer, she'd refused, saying that if they absolutely had to bring the letters into the equation to save the house, then they would. But for now, they'd see what happened with the State Review Board, and they'd move on with the originally planned house renovations, which meant that, in a few weeks, they'd be starting on the structural problems. But Dax didn't want to think about all the work ahead of them right now; this was his wedding day, after all.

"Okay, let's get one of the bride and her family before it gets too dark," the photographer instructed, and Celeste, her parents and Nelsa posed in front of the bounty of twinkling red poinsettias beside the house.

"Beautiful," the photographer said and Dax agreed.

"Yes, she is, isn't she?" He slowly neared his bride, then kissed her softly.

Every touch from Celeste made his insides sizzle with heat…and with need. It'd been her idea to wait until their wedding night to make love again, and Dax had been hard since he woke up this morning merely from thinking about finally having her.

Four weeks had never seemed so long.

As if knowing where his thoughts had headed, she leaned toward him and whispered in his ear, "I can't wait to get out of this dress."

"What a coincidence. I can't wait to get you out of that dress."

She smiled seductively, and Dax grew even harder.

"I'm having a difficult time here, *chère*. Keep teasing me like that, and we might have to leave this party early, head into the house and—"

"I know where I want our first time to be—our first time as husband and wife, that is. And it isn't the plantation."

"Care to enlighten me? Because it better not be far from here. I'm not kidding about how badly I need you, Celeste." He nuzzled her ear, then lowered his voice to a raspy whisper. "I need to feel your naked body against me, to press against your wetness, then slide inside…"

Her gasp was audible, the pulse at her throat quickened and she arched her body against his.

Dax smiled. He'd wanted to see if she was as eager as he was, and she almost seemed more.

She turned her head to look directly at him, and Dax was momentarily spellbound by the green of her eyes. He was still getting used to the vibrant color.

"Celeste, I have a wedding present for you," Nanette said as she neared the two of them.

"I've already got everything I need right here." She rose on her toes and nibbled on Dax's ear. "And I'll have everything I want real soon, won't I?" she whispered to him.

"I won't argue with you," Nan said, not hearing the whispered addition, "but I do have something that I want to tell you about."

"What is it?" Celeste asked, sliding her arm around Dax and massaging his behind.

Enjoying this game, he moved his hand to the small of her back, then dipped it inside her gown to finger the top of her thong.

She giggled softly, but Nanette didn't appear to notice, and plunged on. "I learned at my school's staff meeting this week that Norco Elementary had one of their kindergarten teachers leave at the Christmas break. She's not coming back for the remainder of the year, and they really need to hire someone who can begin as soon as school starts back in January."

"Norco Elementary?" Celeste asked. "Wasn't that the school that Angelle attended? I think I remember her saying that name."

Nan nodded. "It isn't far from here. I thought you might be interested, so I spoke with the principal."

"And?" Dax asked.

"She wants to talk to you whenever it's convenient."

Celeste wrapped her arms around Nanette and

squeezed her. "Oh, Nanette, thank you so much. That's the best wedding present! If I could get a job here, so close to the plantation…well, that'd be a dream come true." She looked at Dax. "*Another* dream come true."

"Well, I didn't get you the job, but I would say that you've got more than a foot in the door. The principal there is a friend of mine, and I think he'll pay special attention to my recommendation."

Celeste's eyes were glistening with tears when she turned to Dax. "Isn't that wonderful?"

He nodded, truly enjoying seeing her so happy.

"No way," Nanette mumbled, looking beyond them toward the plantation house.

"What?" Dax asked.

"Roussel. He walked into the house. I guarantee you he's taking advantage of your wedding to snoop around." She slapped her hands together. "Well, we'll just see about that." She stomped off as Dax chuckled.

"The parish president hasn't exactly earned any brownie points with Nan."

"So I see." Celeste watched Nan grab handfuls of her red bridesmaid skirt to get it out of the way as she barreled up the front steps in hot pursuit of her sworn enemy.

"Don't tell her I told you this, but I think she actually enjoys sparring with him. So, I'd say she's still having a good time at our wedding, Charles Roussel or not. In fact, I believe all of my family is having a good time."

His parents, living in a retirement community in Florida now, had driven in for the wedding, and they were currently visiting with his aunts and uncles who had also come back to the plantation for the big event. None of them had seen the place since Katrina, and while they were dismayed at the hit their beloved home had taken—and the fact that their children hadn't called them for help—they'd been impressed that the six cousins currently serving medium duty had pulled together to make things right and were very pleased with all that they had accomplished so far.

Naturally, they'd all pulled out their wallets and offered to foot the bill for repairs, but Nanette had informed them that it was only a matter of time until the historical society came through with funding. Dax knew that the actual amount of time until the money came—if the money came—was unpredictable. But he also knew that Nanette didn't want to ask for help. Truthfully, he didn't either. They would save the house, and they wouldn't take from their parents' retirement money to do it, not unless it was absolutely necessary. Right now, it wasn't necessary.

Dax scanned the yard and saw Gage and Kayla speaking with the caterers, probably scheduling them for their wedding on Valentine's Day. Then he saw Jenee chatting with Monique and Ryan. They waved at him, and he grinned, knowing they were all thrilled that he'd managed to find the woman of his dreams.

He continued scanning the areas under the tents, and then the backyard, but didn't see the other Vicknair cousin.

"Where's Tristan? He didn't get called to a fire, did he?"

"Isn't that him?" Celeste asked, pointing toward the

farthest corner of the back tent, where Tristan's tall frame leaned casually against one of the poles securing the tent, and a striking blonde held his attention. She was standing so close to him that Dax almost didn't recognize her, and he wouldn't have, if the woman hadn't turned her head and smiled.

"Chantelle," Dax said.

"They look pretty—intense," Celeste said.

Dax agreed. The two were definitely in a heated conversation about something…perhaps about each other? "She's the sister of a ghost Gage helped a couple of months ago. Or, I guess I should say a ghost we all helped a couple of months ago, since helping Lillian Bedeau cross was undeniably a joint effort. I wondered back then if Chantelle and Tristan didn't have something between them. They seemed to connect, in a weird kind of way, you know? But the timing wasn't right, of course, with everything she was going through with her sister and all. And they did tend to fight a lot."

"I've seen people like that," Celeste said. "They're either fighting, or making up, and they put everything they've got into both." She laughed. "Some people enjoy relationships like that."

"Not me," Dax said.

"Really, Mr. Vicknair? Well, what kind of relationship do you like? I mean, since I just married you and all, it seems I should probably know."

He moved his mouth back to her ear, kissed that

sweet lobe, then whispered, "I like the kind where I know exactly what a woman wants, because she holds nothing back. I want to know what she's thinking, what she's feeling, what she's needing, in every way. And then I want to fulfill those needs, those wants, those desires. I want to be her best friend, her confidant, but I also want to be the lover who fulfills her every fantasy, her every dream. So when she thinks of having a man, she can think of no other...but me."

"Dax."

He sucked her lobe, then kissed it and blew warm air against her ear. "What do you want, Celeste? You said you knew where you wanted our first time as husband and wife to be. Tell me what you want, and I'll give it to you. Repeatedly."

"The levee."

He smiled against her ear. "Come with me."

They exchanged greetings with guests along their way to the porch, where Dax grabbed two thick quilts from the rockers, draped them over his arm, then helped Celeste gather the train of her gown to descend the stairs. Then they circled the large oak that centered the driveway. Cars were parked around the big tree and lined the entire driveway, and Dax guided his bride to the outer edge of them, along the magnolias that bordered the side.

"We're leaving the party early, aren't we? We *are* the guests of honor, you know," she reminded him with a slight giggle.

"There are plenty of Vicknairs here to keep folks entertained, and tons of champagne," he said, not concerned at all with his guests, and totally concerned with giving his new wife what she wanted.

Once they were away from the lights of the house, Dax noted the full moon and the nice warm breeze blowing from the other side of the levee, where the Mississippi churned. He grinned. There wasn't supposed to be a full moon tonight and he wondered…was this one visible to everyone, or was it placed here, for them, by the powers that be? The breeze was warm enough to keep them comfortable as they made love, and the moon was bright enough that he'd be able to see Celeste's eyes when she came.

"It's perfect, isn't it?" she said from beside him, and he saw that she was staring at the picture before them with awe as well. "Did they do this for us?" She indicated the sky.

"I believe so. And it is close to perfect, but it isn't perfect yet."

"How's that?"

He handed her the quilts and, looking at him questioningly, she held them against her chest. Then he scooped her into his arms. "I told you I'd carry you one day, Mrs. Vicknair."

Laughing, she gathered the flowing length of her dress and piled it on top of the quilts, while Dax carried her down the remaining length of the driveway, then across River Road and up the levee.

He stood her beside him, then laid the quilts on the ground, while Celeste stared out at the water.

"Oh, Dax, look."

Moonlight reflected off of the water and provided a sparkling backdrop for their first time together as husband and wife.

"I want you." She unzipped her dress, let it fall to the ground and stood before him in a lacy white thong, white thigh-high stockings and heels. She wasn't wearing a bra, and her nipples were taut and undeniably aroused.

Dax pulled her against him, pressing her sweet center against the bulge in his pants. "Believe me, *chère*, I want you too."

Her hands trembled as she removed his tuxedo jacket, then unbuttoned his shirt. Then she paused. "Dax?"

"Don't tell me you've changed your mind."

She smiled. "No, definitely not. But I'm wondering…"

"What, Celeste?" He waited, and when she didn't say anything, he brought his knuckle beneath her chin and tipped her head so she looked at him directly. "Tell me, *chère*."

"Did you—well, did you bring protection?"

He nodded. "I did."

Then she smiled, but it didn't reach her eyes, and Dax thought he knew why.

"But…" he started.

"But?"

"But if you'd rather not use it, I can't think of

anything better than having nothing at all between us when we make love."

Even in the moonlight, Dax could see the green of her eyes intensify. "You mean, just this time? Our first time? Or do you mean…"

"What do you want, Celeste?" he asked, believing he knew, but wanting to hear her say it.

She smiled broadly. "I think a boy first, but a girl would be fine too. And if it's a boy, I'd like to name him Ike."

Dax's laugh rolled freely. "Ike it is." He skimmed his hands down her hips and slid her panties down her legs.

"Yes," she whispered as his fingers slid between her folds to find her hot, wet and ready. "And, if—it's a girl," she continued, though her words were rasping and hoarse, "Adeline."

She spread her legs to give him better access, while her hands moved to undo his pants, then found his erection and stroked him tenderly. "You know," she panted, "it may take lots of practice to get little Ike or Adeline. I wouldn't want you to get discouraged and give up."

"Oh, don't worry, *chère*. Vicknairs *never* give up."

* * * * *

For a sneak preview of Marie Ferrarella's
DOCTOR IN THE HOUSE,
coming to NEXT in September,
please turn the page.

He didn't look like an unholy terror.

But maybe that reputation was exaggerated, Bailey DelMonico thought as she turned in her chair to look toward the doorway.

The man didn't seem scary at all.

Dr. Munro, or Ivan the Terrible, was tall, with an athletic build and wide shoulders. The cheekbones beneath what she estimated to be day-old stubble were prominent. His hair was light brown and just this side of unruly. Munro's hair looked as if he used his fingers for a comb and didn't care who knew it.

The eyes were brown, almost black as they were aimed at her. There was no other word for it. Aimed. As if he was debating whether or not to fire at point-blank range.

Somewhere in the back of her mind, a line from a B movie, "Be afraid—be very afraid…" whispered along the perimeter of her brain. Warning her. Almost against her will, it caused her to brace her shoulders. Bailey had to remind herself to breathe in and out like a normal person.

The chief of staff, Dr. Bennett, had tried his level best to put her at ease and had almost succeeded. But an air of tension had entered with Munro. She wondered if Dr. Bennett was bracing himself as well, bracing for some kind of disaster or explosion.

"Ah, here he is now," Harold Bennett announced needlessly. The smile on his lips was slightly forced, and the look in his gray, kindly eyes held a warning as he looked at his chief neurosurgeon. "We were just talking about you, Dr. Munro."

"Can't imagine why," Ivan replied dryly.

Harold cleared his throat, as if that would cover the less than friendly tone of voice Ivan had just displayed. "Dr. Munro, this is the young woman I was telling you about yesterday."

Now his eyes dissected her. Bailey felt as if she was undergoing a scalpel-less autopsy right then and there. "Ah yes, the Stanford Special."

He made her sound like something that was listed at the top of a third-rate diner menu. There was enough contempt in his voice to offend an entire delegation from the UN.

Summoning the bravado that her parents always claimed had been infused in her since the moment she first drew breath, Bailey put out her hand. "Hello. I'm Dr. Bailey DelMonico."

Ivan made no effort to take the hand offered to him. Instead, he slid his long, lanky form bonelessly into the chair beside her. He proceeded to move the chair ever so slightly so that there was even more space between them. Ivan faced the chief of staff, but the words he spoke were addressed to her.

"You're a doctor, DelMonico, when I say you're a doctor," he informed her coldly, sparing her only one frosty glance to punctuate the end of his statement.

Harold stifled a sigh. "Dr. Munro is going to take over your education. Dr. Munro—" he fixed Ivan with a steely gaze that had been known to send lesser doctors running for their antacids, but, as always, seemed to have no effect on the chief neurosurgeon "—I want you to award her every consideration. From now on, Dr. DelMonico is to be your shadow, your sponge and your assistant." He emphasized the last word as his eyes locked with Ivan's. "Do I make myself clear?"

For his part, Ivan seemed completely unfazed. He merely nodded, his eyes and expression unreadable. "Perfectly."

His hand was on the doorknob. Bailey sprang to her feet. Her chair made a scraping noise as she moved it back and then quickly joined the neurosurgeon before he could leave the office.

Closing the door behind him, Ivan leaned over and whispered into her ear, "Just so you know, I'm going to be your worst nightmare."

Bailey DelMonico has finally
gotten her life on track, and is
passionate about her recent career
change. Nothing will stand in the way
of her becoming a doctor...that is,
until she's paired with the sharp-tongued
Dr. Ivan Munro.

Watch the sparks fly in

Doctor in
the House

by *USA TODAY* Bestselling Author

Marie Ferrarella

Available September 2007

Intrigued? Read more at
TheNextNovel.com

HARLEQUIN®

Mediterranean NIGHTS™

Sail aboard the luxurious Alexandra's Dream and experience glamour, romance, mystery and revenge!

Coming in October 2007...

AN AFFAIR TO REMEMBER

by

Karen Kendall

When Captain Nikolas Pappas first fell in love with Helena Stamos, he was a penniless deckhand and she was the daughter of a shipping magnate. But he's never forgiven himself for the way he left her—and fifteen years later, he's determined to win her back.

Though the attraction is still there, Helena is hesitant to get involved. Nick left her once...what's to stop him from doing it again?

REQUEST YOUR FREE BOOKS!

2 FREE NOVELS
PLUS 2
FREE GIFTS!

HARLEQUIN®

Blaze®

Red-hot reads!

YES! Please send me 2 FREE Harlequin® Blaze® novels and my 2 FREE gifts. After receiving them, if I don't wish to receive any more books, I can return the shipping statement marked "cancel." If I don't cancel, I will receive 6 brand-new novels every month and be billed just $3.99 per book in the U.S., or $4.47 per book in Canada, plus 25¢ shipping and handling per book and applicable taxes, if any*. That's a savings of at least 15% off the cover price! I understand that accepting the 2 free books and gifts places me under no obligation to buy anything. I can always return a shipment and cancel at any time. Even if I never buy another book from Harlequin, the two free books and gifts are mine to keep forever.

151 HDN EF3W   351 HDN EF3X

Name	(PLEASE PRINT)

Address	Apt.

City	State/Prov.	Zip/Postal Code

Signature (if under 18, a parent or guardian must sign)

Mail to the **Harlequin Reader Service®:**
IN U.S.A.: P.O. Box 1867, Buffalo, NY 14240-1867
IN CANADA: P.O. Box 609, Fort Erie, Ontario L2A 5X3

Not valid to current Harlequin Blaze subscribers.

Want to try two free books from another line?
Call 1-800-873-8635 or visit www.morefreebooks.com.

* Terms and prices subject to change without notice. NY residents add applicable sales tax. Canadian residents will be charged applicable provincial taxes and GST. This offer is limited to one order per household. All orders subject to approval. Credit or debit balances in a customer's account(s) may be offset by any other outstanding balance owed by or to the customer. Please allow 4 to 6 weeks for delivery.

Your Privacy: Harlequin is committed to protecting your privacy. Our Privacy Policy is available online at www.eHarlequin.com or upon request from the Reader Service. From time to time we make our lists of customers available to reputable firms who may have a product or service of interest to you. If you would prefer we not share your name and address, please check here. ☐

HB07

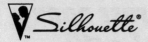

Romantic
SUSPENSE

Sparked by Danger,
Fueled by Passion.

When evidence is found that Mallory Dawes
intends to sell the personal financial information
of government employees to "the Russian,"
OMEGA engages undercover agent Cutter Smith.
Tailing her all the way to France, Cutter is
fighting a growing attraction to Mallory while at
the same time having to determine her connection
to "the Russian." Is Mallory really the mouse in
this game of cat and mouse?

Look for

Stranded with a Spy

by *USA TODAY* bestselling author

Merline Lovelace

October 2007.

Also available October wherever you buy books:

BULLETPROOF MARRIAGE *(Mission: Impassioned)*
by Karen Whiddon

A HERO'S REDEMPTION *(Haven)* by Suzanne McMinn

TOUCHED BY FIRE by Elizabeth Sinclair

Visit Silhouette Books at www.eHarlequin.com   SRS27553

HARLEQUIN®

Blaze™

COMING NEXT MONTH

#351 IF HE ONLY KNEW... Debbi Rawlins
Men To Do
At Sara Wells's impromptu farewell party, coworker Cody Shea gives her a sizzling and unexpected kiss. Now, he may think this is the end, but given the hidden fantasies Sara's always had about the hot Manhattan litigator, this could be the beginning of a long goodbye....

#352 MY FRONT PAGE SCANDAL Carrie Alexander
The Martini Dares, Bk. 2
Bad boy David Carrera is the catalyst Brooke Winfield needs to release her inner wild child. His daring makes her throw off her conservative upbringing...not to mention her clothes. But will she still feel that way when their sexy exploits become front-page news?

#353 FLYBOY Karen Foley
A secret corporate club that promotes men who get down and dirty on business travel?
Once aerospace engineer Sedona Stewart finds out why she isn't being promoted, she's ready to quit. But then she's assigned to work with sexy fighter pilot Angel Torres. And suddenly she's tempted to get a little down and dirty herself....

#354 SHOCK WAVES Colleen Collins
Sex on the Beach, Bk. 2
A makeover isn't exactly what Ellie Rockwell planned for her beach vacation. But losing her goth-girl look lands her a spot on her favorite TV show...and the eye of her teenage crush Bill Romero. Now that they're both adults, there's no end to the fun they can have.

#355 COLD CASE, HOT BODIES Jule McBride
The Wrong Bed
Start with a drop-dead-gorgeous cop and a heroine linked to an old murder case. Add a haunted town house in the Five Points area of New York City, and it equals a supremely sexy game of cat and mouse for Dario Donato and Cassidy Case. But their staying one step ahead of the killer seems less dangerous than the scorching heat between them!

#356 FOR LUST OR MONEY Kate Hoffmann
Million Dollar Secrets, Bk. 4
One minute thirty-five-year-old actress Kelly Castelle is pretty well washed-up. The next she's in a new city with all kinds of prospects—and an incredibly hot guy in her bed. Zach Haas is sexy, adventurous...and twenty-four years old. The affair is everything she's ever dreamed about. Only, dreams aren't meant to last....

www.eHarlequin.com

HBCNM0907